T0064896

BLACK THUNDER

BLACK THUNDER

THREE CLASSIC WESTERNS

by

MAX BRAND

SKYHORSE PUBLISHING

CONTENTS

Lawman's Heart

Frederick Faust published twelve serials and twenty-five short fictional works in 1934, in a variety of publications, including *Harper's Magazine, Argosy, Collier's,* and Street & Smith's *Western Story Magazine,* this last his primary and almost sole market from 1922 until 1932. "Lawman's Heart" was one of the seven short novels that appeared in *Star Western* in 1934. It was published under the Max Brand byline in the May issue.

I

The place looked safe and it felt safe. The stagecoach had come in sight of its destination at Little Snake. The passengers could wipe the dust from their faces and see the wriggle and flash of the river that crossed the flat and split the town in two. Heat waves dimmed the mountains, and danced over the strata of vari-colored rocks across the flat range. The whole scene was one of peace and somnolence.

Young Larry Traynor, in the driver's seat, knotted his brows a little as he prepared to sweep the stage down the cataracting slopes that led into the flat below. Certainly there was no thought of danger in his mind. He had a good set of brakes and he had a pair of excellent leaders. He hardly needed the long reins to drive them. His voice was enough, and they pulled wide or close according to the curves they encountered.

Besides, when Larry Traynor came in view of Little Snake, something moved like music in his blood, a happy sadness, as he thought of Rose Laymon. Once she had been close to him, but time and another man had put a distance between them, and now there was only the melancholy beauty of his memories.

The stage was rolling over the last of the upgrade and lurched onto the level. Traces and chains loosened. Traynor was about to call to the leaders when a voice barked from a clump of brush inside the curve of the road. The sound of that voice, shrill and piercing, scattered the sleepy unreality of the moment. A long rifle barrel gleamed through the brush; a masked head rose into

3

view, sleek black cloth with white showing through the eye slits.

Sam Whitney, the veteran guard who shared the driver's seat with Traynor, muttered—"The damn' rat . . . ."—and jerked up the double-barreled, sawed-off shotgun that was always under his hand.

He got halfway up from his seat before the rifle spoke. There was no flame, no smoke—just the shiver of the barrel and the clanging noise. Sam Whitney kept on leaning forward. He threw the rifle before him. He fell from the seat as the stage lurched to a stop under the brakes that Traynor had thrown on.

Traynor saw the body of his old friend hit the rump of the off-wheeler. He saw a spray of blood fly. Then Whitney, turning in the air, landed with a solid impact in the road. Sam Whitney lay flat on his back in the dust of the road, and stared up at the glare of the afternoon sky.

Traynor could only see that picture. He hardly heard the shrill voice that commanded the passengers out of the coach. It was a strange voice, too high and sharp to be real. Only something in the subconscious mind of Traynor kept his hands stretched high above his head. Vaguely he was aware that the passengers had their arms high over their heads, also, and that one man was obeying the commands of the robber to throw things out of the boot. There was money back there—more than $20,000.

The robber held his rifle under the hollow of his arm while he accepted the canvas sack in his other hand. The passengers faced him in a line. If they tried to follow him, they would catch hell, the masked man told them. The sun glinted for the last time on the rifle as he backed into the brush. The green leaves swayed together. The fellow was gone.

And still Traynor sat for a rigid moment with the arms stuck up high above his head. His heart had leaped up into his throat and trembled there, beating too fast for a count. For the last three months, whenever a moment of excitement came, his heart acted like that, paralyzing his body.

4

Nerves, he told himself. The old woman in him was coming out. Suddenly he could move; he could think. He sprang down into the road and knelt in the dust.

"Sam! Hey, Sam!" he called.

Out of the babel of voices of men congratulating one another that the robber had not stripped them of watches and wallets, Traynor heard one fellow saying: "He killed the guard, all right."

"Almighty God," said Traynor.

He could not believe it. Dead men should stare at the world with dead eyes. But there was still the old twinkle of humor in the look of Sam Whitney, just as when he stood at a bar, resting one foot on the rail, hurrying through an anecdote before he swallowed his drink. Now Sam's expression looked as if he were just going to make some humorous retort to the last speaker.

"'Possums taught me how to play dead," he'd say.

But he said nothing. His eyes would not move from the distance into which they peered. And there was a great red blotch across his breast.

Traynor ran for the buckskin leaders. He had a revolver with him. Fool that he was, he could remember now that he was armed.

He cut the near leader out of its harness, leaped on the bare back, and raced the horse into the brush, up the slope. His passengers howled after him. Their voices were no more to Traynor than sounds of the journeying wind.

Sam Whitney was dead! And there never would be peace in Traynor's soul until the murderer went down. Old Sam Whitney had taught him how to throw a rope. Old Sam Whitney—why, he had always been old, even when Traynor was only a child. He had taught Traynor how to strum a guitar. And how to shoot. And how to stick to the back of a pitching bronco.

"If you're feeling sick, maybe that damned mustang will be feeling a lot sicker," Sam Whitney used to say. He had taught Traynor how to fight. "The other fellow looks good when he's hitting . . . he looks damn' bad when he's being hit. Bulldog, bulldog is the trick."

Sam Whitney was dead, but part of his soul would live on in the minds of his friends, and in the mind of Larry Traynor above all. Bulldog—that was the thing.

The buckskin, running like a racer, blackened with sweat already, streaked across the round forehead of the mountain, through trees, into the clear. And yonder galloped a big man on a swift little horse, a quick-footed little sorrel. A mountain man on a mountain horse, no doubt.

The robber turned, the black mask of his face with the white showing through the eye holes. He snatched up his rifle. And Traynor, as the buckskin ran in, fired twice.

The first bullet hit empty air, and he knew it. The second shot skidded the sombrero off the head of the robber. Then the rifle spoke and the buckskin fell on its nose.

Traynor turned a somersault, got staggeringly to his feet, and fired once more at a dim vision that was disappearing through the thick of the brush. The only answer that came back to him was the clattering of hoofs that disappeared into the distance.

He turned to the buckskin. The bullet had clipped it right between the eyes. Beautiful shooting! Shooting almost too beautiful, because there were not half a dozen men in the mountains who were able to make a snap shot as effective as this. Such accuracy narrowed the field in which he would have to search.

He stripped the bridle and harness from the limp, dead buckskin. Then Traynor went over to the spot where the sombrero had fallen. It was a common enough hat—a Stetson—and he looked at the sweat band, where initials of owners are often punctured through the leather, but there was no sign. The hat was new, which made it all the worse as an identifying mark. He tried it on his head. It was a perfect fit, and that made him sigh with a greater despair.

However, he had something to go on. A mountain man riding a sorrel mountain horse, an active little beauty—a fellow who was a dead shot. Or had that bullet been intended for the breast of Traynor when the tossing head of the mustang intercepted its course? As well be hunted for two murders as for one.

Thoughtfully Traynor walked over the round of the slope and back into the road. The passengers started chattering at him. At least they had had the decency to put the dead body of Sam Whitney back into the coach. Someone had closed his eyes.

"No luck," said Traynor gloomily. "This hat, and that's all." He put the other buckskin leader behind the stage and drove down the sloping road with only four horses, the pointers acting bewildered when they found themselves at the head of the team.

* * * * *

They entered Little Snake. A crowd, half mounted and half running on foot, was already tailing about the stage, shouting questions when the fattest and oldest man among the passengers called: "There's Bill Clancy's clothing store! Stop over there and see if he might have sold this hat."

Traynor stopped the coach. The crowd fell on the passengers. Half a dozen attached themselves to each man, babbling questions, getting terse, important answers. When they got into Clancy's store, they first stood at the counter with proprietarial airs, waiting for Clancy to finish examining the hat.

He was a sour-faced little man, this Clancy, and now he took the Stetson on the tip of his finger and caused it to rotate slowly under his eyes. His hands were pale, clean, delicately shaped. He had the air of the artist examining a mystery, and a beautiful mystery, at that. He turned the hat over, regarded the sweat band, which was only slightly darkened toward the front.

"The gentleman who wore this hat," pronounced Mr. Clancy, "did not sweat a whole lot around the forehead." He turned down the leather sweat band and looked inside it.

"Gentlemen," he said, "I sold this hat." There was a little grunting sound from the whole crowd, as if they had all been in a conveyance and had gone over a jolting bump. Traynor began to feel cold about the lips.

"I sold this hat," said Clancy, "and the name of the gentleman to whom I sold it was . . . ." He paused, studying something that caught his attention. "I always write in the initials of the purchaser," murmured Clancy, in the midst of his thought. "These initials are rubbed a little dim, but . . . yes . . . this is the hat that I sold to Doctor Parker Channing three weeks ago on Tuesday."

No one spoke. There were good reasons for the silence. Sleek and handsome young Parker Channing had come to Little Snake three months ago on his way to the mountains for a shooting trip. But he found a dozen cases suddenly ready for him and not another physician within fifty miles to rival him.

He lingered on to do his professional duty, then he settled down for an indefinite stay. His reputation was carried on the wings of the wind. When he operated on the skull of Tim Wallace and saved Tim's life or reason, or both, by removing a segment of the bone, his skill as a surgeon was established. And when he saved the wife of Big Joe Mellick from death by typhoid, it was apparent that he was an exceptional medical man, also. If his prices were high, his services were worth it.

He became at one stride the leading professional man of the town. He was an honor to it. He could stick to the back of a bucking mustang as well as the next fellow. He could shoot circles around nearly every man in the district when it came to a hunting party. He was the best of company, had a tight head to hold whiskey, and was such an all-around prize that it was little wonder that he took the eye of the prettiest girl in town. He walked her away from Larry Traynor the very first time he met her.

And that was why most heads in the Clancy store now turned suddenly toward Traynor—not because it was his dear friend who had been murdered, but because it seemed apparent that Dr. Channing was the murderer.

Clancy could not fail to rise to a situation of this magnitude. He leaned across the counter and offered the Stetson to Traynor. "I guess you'll be wanting to give this hat back to the gent that owns it, Larry."

Give it back to the handsome doctor? Perhaps receive some lead out of the doctor's gun in exchange? Traynor accepted the dangerous mission with his eyes on the floor. His heart was up there in his throat again. He could not move; he could not speak. A strange, dizzy sense of faintness was sickening him. Then he thought of the dead man and lifted his head suddenly. "I'll look up Doctor Channing," he said.

II

The stagecoach had to be taken to the station. The passengers left Clancy's store with Traynor, and he drove at a dog-trot back to headquarters.

Abe Terry, the general manager of the line, sat on the bench before the station stable whittling a stick and spitting tobacco juice into the deep dust of the street. He did not move to avoid the cloud of white dust that blew over him. He merely lifted his head a little to watch the men who took off their hats before they carried the dead man into the building. He was whittling again and working at his quid when Traynor came up to him.

"Yeah, I've heard," said Abe Terry. "Gonna have a chat with the doctor?"

"I'm going to have a chat with him," agreed Traynor.

"He'll shoot hell right out of you," said Abe thoughtfully.

"Yeah, and maybe he won't."

"It's your party," said Abe, "but why not wait till the sheriff gets in? He's due sometime this afternoon."

"If I can find the doctor, I'm going to have it out with him," said Traynor.

"Well, more power to you. Watch both his hands. The sucker is as good with his left as with his right, they tell me. He's over at the Laymon house on the front porch, chewin' the fat with Rose."

Traynor nodded. "Supposing that anything happens," he said, "put this ten bucks on old Sam, will you?"

Abe Terry took the greenback and fingered it. "What the hell good will ten bucks do Sam now?" he asked.

"Flowers, or something," said Traynor.

"Yeah. Flowers or . . . what the hell?"

"Turn it into coffee and limburger, or whiskey for the drunks that are broke," said Traynor. "It comes from Sam. That's all."

"Owe him this?" asked Abe.

"More than that. I owe Sam millions."

"Oh, that's the way, is it?" said Terry. And he spat into the dust again. "Fond of the old goat, were you? Look here, Larry. Why be a damn' fool? Why not wait till the sheriff gets home?"

"If I were the fellow that lay cold," said Traynor, "Sam wouldn't wait for any sheriff."

"Well, go on and play your hand," said Abe Terry. "I'm wishing you luck. Remember, if you start shooting from the hip, you're likely to pull to the right. I always noticed that. I pulled a gun on a Canuck down in Flaherty's saloon, once, and I shot a bottle off the bar right beside his left arm. Then he put a dose of lead inside my hip and turned me into a lame duck for the rest of my life." He waved his hand. "So long, Larry."

"So long, Abe."

The Stetson was still in the hand of Traynor. As though it were a flag, it called people toward it. There were a half a hundred men and boys walking around the block after him toward the Laymon house.

The men sauntered at ease, each fellow pretending that his way simply happened to coincide with that of Traynor. But they kept advising the boys to get back out of the way of possible trouble. It came over Traynor that he would certainly be left alone to start the trouble with the doctor. The crowd would hold back.

Not that the men were cowards. There in Little Snake lived as many brave fellows as one could wish to see, but Traynor had a special purpose in enforcing this arrest and the crowd would hold back and let him make his try. If he failed—well, even then nothing might be done. The law ought to take care of its own troubles, and the sheriff was the law in Little Snake.

The Laymon house hove in view. It was two tall stories high and had a whole block of trees and garden around it. John Laymon never did things by halves. Thirty miles out from town he had one of the best ranches in the valley, crowded with fat cattle. But he preferred to keep his family closer to the stageline.

Money had come to John Laymon through his patient labor and keen brain. Reputation had come to him some three or four years ago when he had rounded up the entire Wharton gang of rustlers who had been preying on the cattle of the community. He had brought in the sheriff, raised a force of fighting cowpunchers, contributed his own wise head and steady hand, and they had scooped up the gang and sent the Whartons to prison. After that, John Laymon spent less of his time on his distant ranch that lay back among the mountains in a fertile valley. He was more often in town.

But he was not in sight as Traynor advanced toward the house. There was only Rose Laymon in a white dress and the doctor. Her arms were bare; her throat was bare. She was as brown as a schoolboy, and Traynor could guess at the blue of her eyes long before he actually could see the color.

She was small and slender, but her wrists and her arms and her throat were rounded. Traynor could see the flash of her laughter from the distance, and then he turned in up the path under the big shade trees.

The crowd waited behind him. Some of the men leaned on the fence and some remained clear across the wide, treeless street.

The doctor lounged in a chair near the girl. He wore gray flannels and a white shirt open at the throat, without a necktie. There was no other man in Little Snake who would have dared to wear such clothes—not even Clancy himself. But the doctor had no fear. He wore white shoes, too, and he had his legs crossed and swung one lithe foot up and down.

When he saw Traynor coming with the hat, however, he began to straighten himself in the chair, little by little. He was big and he was lean; he was supple and quick; he had the look of a fellow who might be capable of almost any physical exertion, and as a matter of fact he was as good as his looks.

But what depressed Traynor more than all else was the great sweep of the intellectual brow above that handsome face. The doctor had everything from education to brains. It was not at all strange that he had taken Rose away from Traynor at a gesture. What was Traynor in comparison but a rather stodgy figure, a common cowpuncher not even distinguished for skill with a rope or a branding iron?

He was merely "one of us", and people like the doctor always ride herd on the ordinary men. The immensity of the gulf between him and the murder kept widening in the understanding of Traynor as he drew closer. He could see himself as a mere pawn contrasted with a king among men. It seemed to him miraculous that he, Larry Traynor, could ever have sat on that verandah at the side of Rose Laymon.

He went up the front steps, one at a time, tipping his hat to the girl. He took his hat clear off. Sweat began to run on his hot forehead. He raised his left arm and wiped the sweat off on the flannel sleeve of his shirt.

The girl stood before him, saying coldly: "Do you want something . . . Larry?"

She had started to say mister, and then shame, perhaps, had stopped her. But he could forgive pride in such a girl. Let the pretty women pick and choose because, once they have chosen, they settle down to trouble enough.

"I want to give this hat back to the doctor," he said. He offered it, with a gesture.

Parker Channing sat forward, rose. He took the hat in a careless hand, examined it. "I never saw it before," he said.

"No?" said Traynor. His heart was beginning to rise in his breast, stifling him.

"No, I never saw it before," said the doctor.

"What's this all about?" asked the girl. "Why do you look at Parker with such a terrible eye, Larry?"

"Because I was wondering . . . ." Traynor breathed. "I was wondering whether or not he was a murderer."

The girl made two or three quick steps back. She put out a slim hand against the wall of the house. The heat had crumpled the white paint to roughness.

"Don't pay any attention, Parker," she said. "He's simply drunk again."

That was the way she had been talking to the doctor about him then? A town drunkard—was that what she had been making of him?

"I won't pay too much attention to him," said the doctor. "He's not drunk, though he looks like it."

His gaze suddenly narrowed, became professionally curious. It fastened like teeth on the throat of Traynor. A malicious interest gleamed in his eyes. What could he see?

"A man wearing this hat," said Traynor, "held up the stage I was driving and shot old Sam to death."

"Not Sam!" cried the girl. "Oh, Larry, not old Sam!"

"Yes. He's dead."

"But he can't be. Only two days ago . . . ." She stopped. Something was passing between the two men that locked up her speech in ice.

"The murderer was wearing this hat. You never saw the hat before, Doctor?"

"Never," said Channing. "Sorry to hear about . . . ."

"You're sorry, are you?" muttered Traynor. There was rage in him to warm his blood, but always there was that horrible fluttering of his heart, and the need to gasp wider for air. "You never even saw this Stetson before?"

"I've told you that before, man. What's the matter with you?" asked Parker Channing coldly.

"Your initials are inside the sweat band, where Clancy wrote them in when he sold you this hat three weeks ago Tuesday."

The doctor's head jerked back. His right hand darted inside his coat.

"No, Parker!" cried the girl. "No, no!"

Traynor's grip was on the butt of his Colt. He did not draw it. There seemed no strength to draw the gun. He knew, by the cold of his face, that he was deadly white. His eyes ached, they thrust out so hard. And there came over him the frightful surety that he was a coward.

He could not believe it. He had gone through his troubles—not many of them, but he had faced what all Westerners have to face—half-mad horses under the saddle, high dangerous trails, and sometimes an argument with an armed drunkard in a saloon. Yet here he found himself hardly able to breathe, and the tremor from his heart had invaded his entire body.

"You don't mean that he's right," moaned Rose Laymon. "It's not really your hat, Parker?"

The doctor, breathing hard, swayed a little back and shook his head. "No . . . not mine. At least, if it is mine, then someone else stole it. I don't know anything about this murder . . . ."

He was always as cool as steel. But now the coolness was gone. The guilt withered and puckered his face, narrowed his eyes. What was he seeing, briefly, in the distance of time? All the high promise of his life falling in ruins? And in the presence of the girl he had wanted to marry.

"Ah, damn your rotten heart!" said the doctor, and walked straight up to Traynor.

It was the time to stand on guard, but Traynor's arms were lead. The figures before him shifted, were raised from their places, wavered in the thin air. The brightness of the sun was gone. He could no longer feel the beating of his heart. His lungs labored, but the life-giving air would not enter them, it seemed. He could hear a rasping, quick pulse of sound and knew that it came out of his own throat.

The doctor struck him across the face and leaped back half a step, his hand inside his coat, half crouched, on edge to draw.

"You lying dog!" said Dr. Channing.

And Traynor could not move.

"How horrible," he heard the girl whisper.

And, far away on the street, where the men of the town were watching, Traynor heard a deep, groaning noise. Nothing as shameful as this had ever been seen in Little Snake.

Cowards have been known to faint in a crisis. And Traynor wanted to faint; he wanted to lie down on the flat of his back and close his eyes and concentrate on the frightful problem of getting enough air into his lungs. Instead, he had to stand, like a wretched, crumbling statue.

The girl walked between him and Channing. "Don't touch him again," she said scornfully. "Whatever you are . . . whatever you've done, Parker, you don't strike a harmless coward a second time."

"Certainly not," said the doctor. "I beg your pardon, my dear. It seems, in fact, that I'm in some trouble, here . . . owing to a little misunderstanding that I'll clear up in no time. Will you trust me to do that?"

She did not answer. She looked as white as Traynor felt. She loved this fellow—this murderer.

"In that case," said Channing, as though he had heard a long and bitter denunciation, "there's nothing to do but say good bye to you forever. And God bless you, Rose. I know you'll mix in a kind thought of me now and again."

He leaned, picked up the Stetson that Traynor had allowed to fall on the porch, and walked down the steps, down the path, out into the open street.

"Gentlemen," he said slowly, tonelessly, "what is it that you will have of me?"

III

He stood out there in the sun with his hat raised, waiting, and running his eye up and down the men of Little Snake, and not a voice answered, and not a hand was raised. He turned his back, and walked without hurrying down the street, and around the corner.

He was well out of view before a murmur grew out of the crowd. It increased to a loud humming. Then a yell broke out of one man. It was echoed by another. The whole crowd lurched suddenly into pursuit of Parker Channing, as fast as their feet would carry them.

"You look sick," said the cold voice of the girl to Traynor.

"I'm all right," he said. He was not at all sure that he could walk, but he managed to get down the steps with sagging knees. When he stood on the level of the path, he turned to do his manners and lift his hat to Rose Laymon. But she was oblivious to him. She had her hands folded at the base of her throat. Her face was not contorted by sobbing, but tears ran swiftly down her cheeks and splashed over her hands.

She loves him, thought Traynor to himself. *She'll never stop loving him. And . . . I wish to God that I were dead.*

He got out from the grounds of the Laymon house, at last, and turned into the emptiness of that wide street. He had to take short steps. His feet would not fall in a straight line but wandered a little crazily. Something akin to nausea worked in his vitals. Something was dead in him.

A pair of boys dashed on ponies around a corner. When they saw him, they reined in their horses. They swept about him in flashing arcs. The hoofs of their ponies lifted a cloud of dust that obscured Traynor.

"Yeller . . . yeller . . . yeller!" they shouted. "Larry Traynor's yeller!" They screamed and they sang the insult.

That was all right, and he might have done the same thing, at their age. The thing was true. He *was* yellow. And yet he still felt that it was the sick breathlessness rather than actual terror that had kept his hands idle back there on the verandah of the Laymon house. All cowards, of course, would have the same feeling. They were not afraid. No, no! They were just troubled with a touch of ague. They felt a mastering chill up the spine. They could not help growing absent-minded because they were thinking about home and mother.

He could have laughed. Instead, he had to start gasping for air in real earnest. Something was profoundly wrong with him. And the two young devils kept wheeling their horses closer and closer to him, yelling more loudly. Other children were coming from the distance. Better ask mercy from Indians than from these mannerless savages.

He saw the little house of the sheriff, unpainted, with nothing except the long hitching rack in what might have been a garden patch. He turned in and climbed the verandah with weary legs.

"Look at him! He's afraid! Coward, coward, coward!" screamed the boys. "Oh, what a coward! He's yeller! Larry Traynor's yeller!"

Traynor pushed the door open—it was never locked—and walked into the tiny, two-room house. Kitchen/dining room—and then a small bedroom.

The sheriff had left in a hurry, this day, for the neatness of his housekeeping was marred by a soiled tin plate on the table and a tin cup with coffee grounds still awash in the bottom of it.

Traynor went into the bedroom and lay down. The blankets held a heavy body odor that seemed to put away the supply of air. He got up wearily and opened the front door and both windows and then the rear door to make a draft. He lay down on the floor of the kitchen and spread out his arms.

Lying on his back did no good. Presently he was sinking. A wavering thread attached him to existence, and the thread was running out, spinning thinner and thinner. To breathe deeply took too much effort. He could only gasp in a profound breath every now and again, when he was stifling.

He turned onto his right side, his head pillowed on his arm. By degrees he felt better. He began to think of old Sam—dead. He began to ride again over the dusty miles the stagecoach had covered. Out of these thoughts he was recalled to himself by the sound of a horse trotting up to the front of the house, the squeak of saddle leather, the thump of feet as a man dismounted.

He sat up. Very strangely, the faintness had left him almost entirely. He rose to his feet, and a moment later the gray-headed sheriff walked into the room.

Compassion entered his eyes when he saw Traynor. Better to be hounded by the insults of the youngsters than to be met by that compassion. But the sheriff shook hands—almost too warmly.

"Sit down, partner," he said. "I'm glad to see you. Mighty glad. I've heard about the stage and everything. A good job you done in skinning away after that crook and getting his hat. We know who the killer is, now, and we'll have a chance to spot him,

one of these days. I'll hit the trail after him right this evening."
He ran on cheerfully: "We've found out what made him do it.
Faro. He couldn't keep away from the game, and Lem Samuels
told us how much he was losing. You can't buy fine horses and
trot a girl all around, and then hit faro, too. So the poor fool
found out about that shipment of cash and decided to help himself. A pretty cool nerve, Larry, when you come to think of it. A
stagecoach filled with armed men and only one . . . ." Here the
sheriff's voice died out, as though he realized he was stepping on
delicate ground.

"I was mighty sorry about old Sam," he said. "One of the best
men in the world . . . and a good friend to you, Larry. I hear the
funeral is tomorrow morning."

"I won't be here," said Traynor. The sheriff waited, and he went
on: "I'll be pretty far out on a trail. And I want to carry handcuffs
with me . . . and a deputy sheriff's badge."

The sheriff whistled softly. He laid his hand on the arm of
Traynor. "Ah, that's it, eh? Good boy, Larry. You were down
for a minute, but the right sort of fellow always comes back. If
you want to go after the doctor, though, hadn't you better go
with me?"

"I'll go alone," said Traynor.

"Got an idea?"

"A piece of one."

"I'll swear you in," said the sheriff. "You know what you're
doing. You shot his hat off once, and I hope to God that you
shoot his head off the next time . . . the damned, murdering,
sneaking rat! Wait till I get a badge for you. . . ."

* * * * *

The outfit that Traynor took was exactly what he wanted—some
dry provisions, a pot and pan, a couple of blankets, a revolver
and a rifle, enough ammunition. But his old horse, Tramper, was

much too high to suit the rider. Tramper had not had much work to do since his master began to drive the stage. He had wandered through rich pasture lands, eating his fill, until his body was sleeked over with fat and his heart was rich with pride. He wanted to dance every foot of the way; he insisted on shying at cloud shadows and old stumps; in the morning he enjoyed working his kinks out with a little fancy bucking.

All of these things would have been nothing to the Traynor of the old days. He would have laughed at the dancing, the shying, the pitching. But the Traynor who survived out of the past was a different fellow. A flurry of hard bucking left him gasping, head down, the landscape whirling before him. And it would be whole minutes before his breath came back to him. Even to sit in the saddle for a few hours was a heavy thing, and he made it a habit to lie down flat beside the trail for a few minutes every couple of hours. Even so, he reached the end of each day almost exhausted.

But a good idea is better than strength to a determined man, and he had the idea. Where would the doctor flee, when he rushed on his fine bay gelding out of Little Snake? Of course he would wish to go far, but what was the greatest distance that he had ever gone from Little Snake through the twisting mountain trails?

A couple of months before, the doctor had been far up on Skunk Creek with a hunting party, and Skunk Creek was a good two days' ride away from the town. It seemed to Traynor a good bet that Channing would head for this distant place among the lonely mountains. From that point of vantage he could plan the rest of his retreat. The sheriff and his men would conscientiously hunt out the sign of the doctor's horse; Traynor preferred to hit far out and take his chance.

The second day was the worst of the two. The altitude made it harder for Traynor. He was continually short of breath. He was continually so very short that he had to gasp like a fish on dry land. About midday, also, he felt discomfort in his feet. By night they were so badly swollen about the ankles that he had to lie with his heels resting on a log higher than his head for a couple of hours before he could reduce the swelling and get his boots off.

On the morning of the third day he simply could not wedge his feet back into the boots. His feet were swelling out of shape. His wrists were heavy, also, and the cursed shortness of breath had increased.

But he was only an hour from the head of Skunk Creek, and he made that distance riding in his socks, his boots strapped on behind the saddle. Something had gotten into his system—some sort of poison, he presumed. And it was settling in the extremities. Some good, hard sweating when he got back into the heat of the valley would probably make all well.

Then he forgot his troubles of the body.

It was the glimmering verge of the day through which he rode; it was only the gray of the early dawn when he came down a gully toward the head of Skunk Creek. He thought, at first, that it was a wisp of morning mist that floated above the head of a cluster of aspens. But the mist kept rising, thin and small, always replenished.

It was fire smoke!

At the edge of the aspens he dismounted and leaned for an instant against the shoulder of the horse. His heart was rocketing in his body. His swollen feet were painful to stand on. His wrists were so thick that the rifle had a strange feeling in his grasp. His eyes felt heavy, too. He could find pouches beneath them by the touch of his fingertips.

He looked for an instant about him. The rose of the morning had entered the gray dawn. The mountains shoved up black elbows against the brilliance of the sky. It was his country, and he loved it. But the beauty of it gave him no joy now. He could think of nothing except the horrible fluttering, the irregular pulsation of his heart, like a flock of birds beating their wings without a steady rhythm.

Was he to be mastered again—if indeed that smoke rose from the campfire of the doctor—not in battle, but by the maudlin weakness of his own spirit? Not spirit, either. Matters of the spirit do not puff the eyes and make the limbs swell.

Somewhere in the back of his mind he kept a sense of the old mountain tales of Indian witchcraft, and of evil spirits breathed into the bodies of condemned men by the ancient seers. It was like that—that was how he felt, exactly. He went on gingerly through the copse.

Now, beyond the thinning of the trees, he could see the silhouette of a man saddling a horse. He drew closer. The veil of the trees thinned, and he found himself looking out on Dr. Parker Channing in person, in the act of drawing a bridle over the head of that lofty bay gelding. The gray flannels and the white shoes looked a good bit absurd in these mountain surroundings, however smart they had seemed in the town. But the air of the doctor had nothing absurd in it.

That lofty head was carried like a conqueror's. The pair of holstered revolvers at the hips was not there for show, and the Winchester worn in a saddle holster would keep its owner fed fat with the best game the mountains could offer.

No matter what Channing had given up, he was not entirely depressed. It was the blue time of the day, of course, and yet he was singing a little to himself.

Something crackled behind Traynor. That fool horse, Tramper, of course, had followed where he was not wanted. He saw a shadowy impression of the animal behind him, and then the doctor was whirling with a drawn revolver.

"Hands up!" yelled Traynor.

"Damn the hands!" said the doctor, and was firing into the trees at what must have been to him a very dim target. Traynor, gun at shoulder, aimed at the breast and fired. He wanted it not this way but another way, but he had to take the game as the doctor chose to play it.

He was certain, as he drew the trigger that his forefinger was closing over the life of big Parker Channing. Then, as the rifle boomed, he heard the clang of the bullet against metal. The revolver, spinning out of the hands of the doctor, arched through the air and struck heavily against the side of the gelding, which went off like a shot down the side of the creek. And out of the woods, squealing like a happy fool, Tramper bolted after this good example of light heels and featherbrain. But Larry Traynor leaned a shoulder against a slender tree trunk and maintained his bead.

"Don't try for that second gun, Doctor," he said.

"Certainly not," said Channing politely. "But can it be my old friend, Traynor? Well met, my lad. Oh, if I'd only had one candlepower more of sunshine to show where you were among those trees."

IV

Fear ought not to choke a man when he had an enemy helpless under a leveled gun. Surely there was no fear in Traynor now, and yet his heart was still swelling in his throat and his breath would not come as he walked out of the woods toward the doctor.

"Unbuckle that gun belt and drop it," he commanded.

The doctor obeyed. His glance was not on the gun, but on the face of the captor. "You're going fast, eh?" he asked.

"Going fast where?" demanded Traynor.

"To hell, old fellow," said the doctor. He kept shifting his glance across the face of Traynor as though he were reading large print. "No, you won't last long," added Channing, as if he were diagnosing a case for a patient.

"Give me your hands," said Traynor.

Channing held them out, and, when he saw the handcuffs, he laughed: "Ah, a legal arrest, eh? No murder, Larry? Just a legal arrest leading up to a trial, and all that?"

Traynor snapped the steel bracelets over the brown wrists of the other. And the doctor sneered openly: "You poor devil! You can hardly breathe, can you?"

"Better than you'll be breathing before many days," said Traynor. "Step back now."

The doctor stepped back. But he kept nodding and smiling, as though he were entirely pleased by what he saw.

Traynor stooped and picked up the fallen gun belt. He strapped it around his own hips.

"I'm curious, Traynor," said the doctor, "just how you managed to know that I'd come here?"

"You'd travel as far as you could over ground that you knew. This is the biggest march you ever made from Little Snake."

The doctor stared. "Well," he muttered, "I'll be damned. Am I as simple as all this? Then I deserve anything that comes to me." And he added, almost with a snarl: "I should have gone the entire way, on the Laymon verandah. I should have drifted lead into you before the other people could see that you weren't able to fight. But here we are . . . what are you going to do?"

"Follow those damned crazy horses, first of all. Face that way and march."

"How far, brother?" asked the doctor, looking down at Traynor's feet, softly muffled in the socks.

"Till I wear the flesh off to the bone!" said Traynor savagely.

"Is that it?" asked Channing. "I'm to be paraded through the streets of Little Snake with the conqueror behind me? Is that it?"

"Something like that," said Traynor. "You're still going to parade into the Little Snake jail. I don't give a damn who sees you go."

"The fact is," said the doctor, rather with an air of curiosity than of concern, "you never would have bothered about me, except that I seem to have shamed you in front of your townsmen?"

"The man you shot off the stage was my best friend," said Traynor. "You had to go down, Doctor. If I could manage to get a chance at you, I would have followed you the rest of my life."

"That wouldn't have been long, old son." The doctor chuckled. He looked again from the swollen feet to the puffed eyes of his captor. "No, that wouldn't have been long."

"Stop bearing down on me," commanded Traynor. "God knows that I'm holding myself hard. I don't want to do you harm, Channing, but if you keep nagging me . . . ."

They followed the two horses a good ten miles. Five of those miles were backtracking completely away from the direction of Little Snake, and, at the end of that distance, from a hilltop Traynor bitterly watched the two animals careening miles and miles away from him down a gulch.

There was little use in following. He could not make the doctor help him catch the horse that was to carry Channing to prison. And Traynor's feet were now in a condition that made walking difficult and running impossible. Gloomily he turned in the direction of far-off Little Snake. "March!" he said huskily.

The doctor laughed, and turned willingly in the appointed direction.

No man thinks of shoes until there is long marching to be done. But Traynor began to yearn for anything that would effectively clothe his feet. He had to cut off slabs of bark and bind them to his feet with strips of clothes, which he sliced into bandages. Other bandages he used to wind around his ankles, and so constrict the swelling. But the puffiness that did not appear in the ankles began higher up in the legs. To walk began to be like wading through mud. Yet through that entire day he kept heading on toward Little Snake.

In the evening he built a fire and stewed some rabbit, which he had shot along the way. They ate that meat. Then the doctor sat with his back to the trunk of a tree and smoked cigarettes, and smiled derisively at his captor.

There was reason and plenty of it for that mockery, as Traynor knew. He had covered a very short distance toward the town. Each day, it seemed, his feet were likely to grow worse and worse. If that were the case, before many days were out he would hardly be able to make perceptible headway.

Presently he said: "Channing, this is a thing to die of, eh?" He pointed to his feet, to his wrists.

"Die of? Why, you're dying now, man," said the doctor. He laughed again. "You were dying down there in Little Snake, and I saw what was the matter with you when I looked at you on the verandah. Dying? You're as good as dead right now."

They were in the green bottom of a gulch, and the doctor looked around him with amused eyes. "And yet," he said, "the medicine is here that will heal you. Make you fit and well again. Right here under your eyes, old son. I'll make the bargain with you. I'll take the swelling out of your legs and wrists . . . out of your whole dropsical body. And in exchange, I'm free to go where I please. What about that? What could be fairer?"

"I'll see you damned first," answered Traynor softly.

Where could the healing stuff be? In the bark of a tree? In roots of grass? In some mineral that the doctor had spotted in some small exposed vein?

"Ignorance is the curse of your people," said the doctor. "You ride your horses, raise your cattle, labor all your lives. Your amusements are drunkenness and gambling. Some of you marry and raise a batch of equally damned children to follow your own dark ways. In the end, men of more intelligence come, exploit the opportunities that you have opened to them, and elbow you out of your holdings. And that is fit and right, Traynor. In the eyes of a superior man, like myself, you and your friend of the driver's seat were no more than wild hogs running loose in the forest."

Traynor gripped his rifle with an instinctive gesture. And then he lay the gun back as suddenly. "No," he said. "That would be the easiest way for you, Channing. Dying wouldn't bother you.

But to be shamed in front of a lot of people . . . to have Rose pitying you and despising you . . . that would be the real hell. And by God, you're going to taste plenty of it before I'm through."

He felt very faint, so he tied the doctor to a tree before he lay down for the night. Afterward, he slept brokenly, and in the earliest dawn he resumed the march, but not for Little Snake. He knew, too, that he could never make the town.

There was a much nearer goal, however. By swinging to the south he would reach the most outlying ranch, the Laymon place, thirty good miles from Little Snake. Once there, his prisoner would be safely in the hands of the law. Old John Laymon, the fiercest of all the enemies of evil-doers, would see to it that Channing was handed over to the sheriff. And the sheriff would see to it that Parker Channing was hanged by the neck till he was dead.

So to the south they marched. At noon, that day, Traynor told himself that he could go no farther. His ankles and wrists had become elephantine. His eyes were puffed until his vision was dim, and inside his breast there was continually that cursed beating as of wings, great and small, in hurried and irregular flight.

If he lay down on his left side, during one of the many rest periods, it seemed to him that he was slipping down, being moved feet first—for the sound of his heart was like the rubbing of two bodies together—like the vibration of a wet finger against a pane of glass. There was constant pain. There was constant faintness.

That night, the huge watery puffing of his flesh suggested something that might ease him. He cut shallow gashes with his knife. Not blood but water flowed out, in quantity. That was a relief, and when the morning came neither his wrists nor ankles seemed to have regained their swollen proportions of the evening before.

Every night, thereafter, he made new incisions, or freshened the old ones so that the water would run out of his flesh. In the middle of the next day's march, the cuts would begin to bleed, blood and water commingled.

His eyes were growing bad, very bad. It was difficult for him to shoot game. Images wavered before him. But on the third day chance enabled him to shoot a deer. Afterward, he could load the prisoner with venison and make him carry the food for the party.

"The worst diet in the world for you, Larry," the doctor said cheerfully. "You're dying, anyway, but you'll die all the sooner under the effects of this diet. Do you want to know how really bad you are? Cut a reed there on the bank of the creek. Put one end to your ear and the other end to your heart. It will be a sort of stethoscope, old son. You can study your death more clearly, that way."

Traynor cut the reed. He was able to bend without breaking it, and with one end to his ear and the other pressed to his breast he listened to the queer, hurrying, faint vibration of his heart. It passed into flurries so rapid and dim that he could not begin to count the contractions. It seemed to him that legions of ghosts were flickering across his vision. And again there were breathless, frightful pauses in which he was sure the next stroke would never come, and at the end of those pauses would come one bell-like stroke that sent a thin shudder all through his being.

He looked up at the sneering, smiling face of the doctor. "Yeah, Parker," he said slowly. "I'm a dying man, all right."

"But why die, you fool?" asked the doctor lightly. "Life all around you . . . plenty to live for . . . and, with what remedies right before your eyes, you might have a long time to go."

Channing began to laugh, blowing out his cigarette smoke in ragged clouds of mirth. "Presently you're going to fall into a coma. That will be the end, Traynor."

"It's true," said Larry Traynor. "I'm going to pass out. You'll brain me with the handcuffs while I'm helpless. And that's why . . . that's why, after all, I have to do this."

"Do what?" asked the doctor cheerfully.

To stand entailed too great an effort. That was why Larry Traynor only pushed himself up to one knee. He raised the rifle and leveled it.

"You have to die, Channing," he said. "I won't be far behind you, I suppose . . . but you'll have to go before me."

"Right," said the doctor. "Either way . . . it makes little difference to me. But what a fool bulldog you are. Blind, stupid, with fat in your brain!"

Down the barrel of the gun, Traynor sighted. He covered the breast. He covered the face. He drew his bead between the bright eyes, just where the bullet had knocked the life out of the buckskin leader.

There was no doubt that the doctor was a brave man, a very brave man. He sat steady enough; he held up his head high, but to look at death is not an easy thing, and, as the seconds ran on, the eyes of Channing began to enlarge and grow too bright.

Suddenly he shouted: "Shoot, damn you!"

Traynor lowered the gun. "I've been trying to. I've been wanting to," he said slowly. "But I can't. I don't suppose I have the nerve to shoot even . . . a dog."

He cast the rifle from him and sat with his head between his hands.

"The poorest fool"—the doctor laughed—"the weakest and the poorest fool that I've ever met."

There was a ridge between them and the valley in which the Laymon house stood. They climbed that ridge. It was only a few miles to go, but it took them four days. Sometimes the dying man walked. Sometimes he crawled. He would hear the doctor say: "Keep your drooling mouth shut, will you?" And then he would realize that he had been walking with his mouth open, babbling meaningless words.

For the agony had ground out his brain. His wits were spinning; he knew that he carried death inside him, in his very heart.

It was on the second day of moiling up that slope that he reached a little pool of still water and looked at his face in the mirror. The thing he saw turned him sick. It could not be his. But when he opened his mouth, the bloated lips of the image also opened.

The doctor said that day: "To do a thing like this for the sake of fame . . . there's sense in that. But to do it for nothing . . . to do it for the sake of a little hand clapping in a village filled with muddy-brained yokels . . . by God, Traynor, I've never heard of such insanity. I'm going to take back some of the other things I've said to you. Whatever else you are, as a bulldog, you're magnificent. You're killing yourself for a crazy sense of justice. What good will the legal murder of me do to the soul of your dead friend? And if you'll make the bargain with me, I'll have you practically fit and well inside of three days. Will you listen to me?"

Traynor did not answer. He was saving his breath because he seemed to need it all. The deadly tremor was entering him more deeply than ever.

They got over the ridge the next day. Below them, Traynor could see the sprawling lines of the ranch house and the barns and the shining tangle of the wire fencing of the corrals. That was the goal, under his eyes, in his hand. It was not three miles away.

It took him five days to cover the three miles, although almost every step of the way was downhill. He did not take so many steps. He was on his knees, waddling, most of the time. Although the knees grew bruised, the mere pain was nothing. The burning of the gashes in his legs helped to keep his wits awake.

He had cut away most of his clothes for bandages, by this time. More than half naked, bloodstained, swollen to a frightful grossness, he could not look down on his body without loathing.

The fourth evening found him still a full mile from the goal. He sat back against a tree, half blind, covering his prisoner constantly with the rifle, although he could only get the tip of a swollen finger inside the trigger guard. And lying there, with an aching throat and a groaning voice, he prayed aloud to God.

He fired shot after shot. He fired them in groups of three, sure signals for help. And yet not a single rider rushed out from the ranch to help him. For four days he had been close enough to catch the attention of some range rider. But when he fired the gun, there was no response—there was only the mocking laughter of the doctor.

But for the fifth day he mustered the last of his strength and the whole exhaustless mass of his courage to bridge the final gap. And it was bridged. Just at the sunset time, that poor, rolling monster and his handcuffed man reached the back door of the ranch house. The steps up the porch seemed to Traynor almost as insurmountable as the Alps.

He shouted, and he had no answer except a feeble echo that flew back to him from the bald, vacant faces of the barns.

Then the doctor said: "I've saved something to tell you. I'll tell it to you now, and be damned to you. I've been crowing over you these five days because, you fool, the ranch is empty! There's nobody in the house. All these five days your bleary eyes couldn't make out the details, but I've seen that not a single soul has left this house or entered it!"

"It can't be empty. It's the Laymon place," mumbled Traynor. "You've got to be wrong . . . you've got to be lying. It's the Laymon place and . . . ."

"If you had something besides death and cotton batting in your brain," shouted the doctor, "you would have noticed that there are no cattle in the fields! Not a damned one. The place has been cleaned out!"

Traynor waited for a moment. He could see very little. Off toward the west there was a redness in the sky, to be sure.

Red—fire—and fire was in his wounds, and the ghastly fog of death was in his brain. So this was the end of the trail, at last.

He said: "Doctor, you ought to die. I wanted to see you hanged."

"Thanks, old son," said the doctor. "I've been appreciating that idea of yours for some days, you know."

"I could chain you here in the house if it's empty, and you'd starve in three days."

The doctor said nothing.

"That wouldn't be pretty, eh? You tied and starving . . . and me spilled out on the floor, my body rotting away before I'm dead. Not pretty, Doctor, eh?"

"My God, no," breathed the doctor.

"Well," said Traynor, "I can't do it. I'll tell you why. I can't help remembering that Rose loved you. I can't do you in like this, Channing." He had to pause and fight for breath.

The captive stared at him with eyes made enormous by wonder.

"Inside this right-hand trousers pocket," said Traynor through his puffed lips, "there's the key to the handcuffs. You take it . . . I can't get my hand into the pocket any more. Take it, and set yourself free." He laid down his gun as he spoke.

The doctor, his hands trembling so that the chain between the handcuffs sang a tuneless song, reached into the pocket and found the key.

And when he had it, he stood over his captor for a moment with his hands raised as though he intended to dash the steel manacles into the hideously distorted face.

Pain in Traynor had reached such a point that he could not fear death itself. That was why he waited for the blow with a frightful caricature of a smile. He felt that this was natural. He had given the tiger its freedom, and the first place the tiger struck would be at him.

But Parker Channing stood back after a moment. He scowled at Traynor. He fitted the key into the lock of the handcuffs; in an instant he was free. He hurled the manacles far away from him, and his glance wandered across the mountains. Freedom and safety lay for him there. The discarded hope of existence returned to him with a rush.

From that prospect, he looked back, suddenly, at the helpless man who lay against the steps of the verandah. The sight made him sneer. As for the bloated, visionless eyes, there was little comprehension in them. To crush Traynor now would be like crushing a toad.

But something else was working in the mind of the doctor. It made him take a few paces up and down, muttering to himself. He wanted to be away. He wanted to be putting miles of safety between himself and the society which waited now only the chance to strangle him at the end of a rope. And still the dim life in the eyes of Traynor held him back.

Channing uttered a final exclamation and stepped away. Traynor looked after him without denunciation, without hope. With the sick man, even the effort of thinking had grown to be almost a physical strain. It was better to lie back and feel the damp cold of the night coming over him. It was better to lie still with the dreadful fluttering in his breast, the movement as of dying wings, wings that have flown to weariness over a sea of darkness into which they must fall. Very shortly, as the night closed over him, his eyes would be closed and never open.

A returning footfall amazed him. Through the dimness he saw the tall form of the doctor go past him, up the steps, across the verandah. A little pause at the door, and Channing entered the house. His footfalls echoed through the emptiness. There was the rattling of iron, iron sounding like that of a stove. Finally the dying man heard the crackling of fire, more cheerful than the song of a cricket. Pans rattled. A fragrance of cookery moved out on the night air.

The doctor was low, a murdering snake without pity or human compassion, but even in him it was peculiar that he should cook for his own comfort while a man lay hungry and dying within sense range of the preparation of the food. The footfalls came loudly out of the kitchen, across the verandah, and descended.

"Stand up!" commanded the doctor harshly.

"No use," muttered Traynor. "If I'm in your way here, roll me out of the path. I'm not moving any more."

"Look," said Channing. "You're rotten. I don't want to touch you. But if you'll try to get up, I'll do something for you."

"Thanks," said Traynor. "And to hell with you, Channing."

The doctor sighed. He leaned down, fitting his strong hands under the shoulders of Traynor, and raised him into a sitting posture. The brain of Traynor whirled dizzily.

"Let me be," he said in a thick husky whisper. "I'm almost finished, Channing. Let me pass out, this way . . . no more pain . . . God! Let it finish off like this downhill . . . ."

The fierce hands of the doctor, strong, hard, painful, ground into his flesh and raised him. He was tottering on his feet. Now he went forward, his huge, hippopotamus feet bumping together as he was more than half lifted up the steps.

The kitchen stove, as they entered the room, he heard roaring with fire. A lamp had been lighted. Wisps of smoke were twisting in the air above the stove, and pans over the fire were trembling a little with the force of the flames. Dim hope, now, entered the mind of Traynor.

The doctor got him down the hall and turned him through a doorway into another lighted room. On the incredible softness of a bed he stretched the body of Traynor. He covered him with blankets.

"Stop thinking," said the doctor, standing over him at last. "Don't do any more thinking. It'll wear out your mind. Look at the light. Remember that you're not going to die."

"Not die?" whispered Traynor.

"No."

"Not die?" murmured Traynor again, and his mouth remained gaping open, as though he were drinking in hope with the air. The doctor left. He returned, after a little, with a cup of tea. He raised the bloated, spongy head of Traynor in the crook of his arm. The tea had a foul odor. The taste of it was green, bitter, sick.

"Pretty bad to swallow, eh?" asked the doctor. "But it's life, Traynor. This is the life that was green all around you, as we came through the valleys. Foxglove, Traynor. It's the plant that doctors get digitalis from. Do you know why your body is almost rotting away from you? It's because your heart has gone bad. And digitalis is going to cure that heart. When the heart is well, you'll be well. You'll be fit for a normal life again. Here . . . finish this stuff off and have some more."

And Traynor drank the foul stuff and almost found it good, it was so sweetened by the taste of hope.

* * * * *

In twenty-four hours the change was incredible. The bloating about the face was almost entirely gone. Traynor's whole body and limbs felt lighter. Above all, he could see clearly; he could think clearly, and, as he stared up at the ceiling, his thoughts led him into a continual maze of wonder.

Channing came back into the room that evening with food, and more of the digitalis tea. Now that his brain and eyes were clearer, he could watch in the face of the doctor the shadow of distaste as he looked down upon the sick man, but mastering that dislike, that horror, there was a keen interest showing through.

He fed Traynor. He held the cup of tea for him, raising his head.

Afterward, he pulled the soggy clothes from the sick man's body and washed him. The exquisite comfort of cleanliness soaked through the flesh, into the soul of Traynor. He had felt too dirty to be worthy of life, or of fighting for it.

And still he wondered, from day to day, as the strength flowed back into his body, into his brain. And the frightful fluttering of wings had left his breast. When he turned on his left side, he could still feel a slight, quick, abnormal vibration, but, otherwise, the beating of the heart did not trouble him except that now and then there would be a great, single drum stroke, as though to give him warning of the condition in which he had once lain.

"The digitalis . . . it's done all this?" he asked, marveling.

The doctor nodded. "It's one of the few drugs that are absolutely necessary to modern medicine. It works miracles. You're one of the miracles. You look like a human being again . . . you are a human being. You're able to sit up. You could start walking tomorrow . . . and that's the day I leave you, Traynor."

Traynor stared upward at the ceiling. "Why did you do this Parker?" he asked.

"I don't know," answered Channing, scowling. "Partly because you were such a bulldog. Partly because . . . well, because the doctor in me was being tormented by the sight of you. My profession is sworn to relieve suffering, you know."

"And you'll be paid for making me well. Do you know how?"

"How?"

"As soon as I can walk and ride, I'm coming on your trail again."

"Good!" exclaimed Parker Channing. "No damned sentimentality. And we'll fight it out to a finish."

"Yes, we will," said Traynor.

He smiled in a strange way at Channing, and Channing smiled in the same manner back at his patient.

"I understand," said Traynor.

"What do you understand?"

"Why it'll be a pleasure to you to cut my throat. It's because you can't stand the idea of me finding Rose Laymon again, and making her forget that the crooked doctor ever lived."

"You'll never make her forget," said the doctor.

"Women know how to put things out of their minds," insisted Traynor.

A patch of white appeared around the mouth of the doctor. "I'll talk no more about it!" he exclaimed, and straightway left the room.

Their understanding was perfect, Traynor knew. They had made a fair exchange. To the doctor he had restored freedom, and the doctor had given him health and life. Neither needed to be grateful to the other. It was a fair exchange and they could part on an equal footing. Yet—except for the picture of old Sam lying on his back in the dust of the road—Traynor knew that he could be fond of this man.

He was simply an outcrop from the ordinary blood of humanity. His brain worked not as the brains of other men operated. There was a greater logic in him, a detached, impersonal coldness of thought. When he was in need of money, therefore, he was able to conceive a crime. Having conceived the crime, he was able to execute it calmly, efficiently, killing the old hero who attempted to interfere with his scheme.

This picture of cold-minded efficiency was marred by only two facts—the real love of the doctor for Rose Laymon, and the human weakness that forced him to tend his worst enemy, curing a patient who would afterward go on the trail to end his life.

These thoughts were in the mind of Traynor that evening; in the morning, the doctor would go, sinking himself deep into the mountains, attempting to secure his freedom from pursuit. And Traynor would wait one day, recovering further strength before he started the long walk back to Little Snake.

He could hear the pounding hoofs of a horse up the road; the doctor was stirring about in the kitchen, singing softly. The sound of the horse turned in toward the ranch house.

Hinges creaked with a great groaning and vibration, as though a wooden gate were being dragged open. After that, noise of hoofs became louder.

The doctor was no longer moving in the kitchen. His step came down the hall. He looked in at the door of the sick man, and Traynor saw the rifle in his hands.

"Somebody's coming. I guess this is good bye, Larry," he said.

"Good luck . . . till I meet you again," said Traynor, smiling thinly.

"The same to you," sneered the doctor, "till I sink lead into you."

The noise of the horse had ended. A footfall sounded on the back porch as the doctor turned to slip away through the front of the house. He was checked by a voice that rang clearly through the old building, calling: "Hello! Who's here? Who's here?"

Channing whirled about as though a knife had dug into him. It was the unforgettable voice of Rose Laymon.

VI

The doctor leaned the rifle against the wall. He looked white, strained, old. "Call her," he whispered to Traynor.

"All right." He lifted his voice. "Rose! I'm in here!"

And the girl answered: "Who . . . Larry Traynor?"

She came running. At the door of the room she halted. The ride had blown color into her face. The hat was well back on her head. And there was such an upwelling of light in her eyes, such a gleaming of surprise and caution and excitement that she looked to Traynor like an Indian girl.

"Larry," she exclaimed, "are you ill? What's the matter? Did you catch up with him? Did that murderer hurt you . . .?"

She was coming into the room, one small step at a time, when she saw the doctor in the corner, among the shadows. She winced from him with an exclamation, as though she had been struck.

The doctor, whiter than ever, made a small gesture. "Murderer is the word, Rose . . . but not a woman killer, you know."

She faced the doctor, but she kept backing up until she was close to the bedside of Larry Traynor. There she put out a small hand, and Traynor took it. He could see an agony in the face of Channing at this gesture that sprang from fear of him. Then the doctor mastered himself. He spoke almost lightly.

"Why not sit down, Rose?" he asked. "I was leaving in the morning, but I'll get out tonight since you've arrived. However, we might all have a chat together."

Her hand wandered behind her, found a chair, drew it toward her while her eyes were still fixed on the doctor. She sat down, close to Larry Traynor.

It seemed as though she had stepped far back in time to the last moment when they had meant so much to one another. With a gesture, in an instant, she had banished the distance that had come between them. And Traynor, turning his own head away from the doctor, watched the breathing of the girl, and his soul extended toward her with an immensity of joy and possession.

"I don't understand it," she said, shaking her head. "Will you tell me what's happened Parker . . . why you're here with Larry, like a friend?"

"He caught me, and slipped the handcuffs on me," said the doctor. He brought out his words with a cool precision. "We're not friends. His heart went bad on the march in. He turned off to this place to shorten the way. He was close to dying when he got here, and, instead of sending me to hell before him, he turned me loose. So I cured his heart trouble for him. We part tomorrow. And we'll meet another day on another trail."

Cold hatred—but respect, too—was in his glance as he stared at Traynor. Yet he went on, forcing himself: "When you and the fools of Little Snake thought that Traynor was showing the white feather the other day . . . that was simply the same heart trouble. I saw the tremble and jump of the pulse, in his throat, and I knew that he was as helpless as a child." He turned to Traynor: "I think this leaves us quits, Larry."

"Absolutely," agreed Traynor.

She almost turned her back on the doctor as she leaned over Traynor. "You know what I thought that day, Larry?" she said. "Yes, because you could see it in my face. Are you going to forgive me?"

"Look," said Traynor. "That didn't happen . . . that's forgotten. The other things . . . what's to come . . . are all that matter."

A slight shadow like the breath of fear ran across her eyes, then she smiled at him. There was that in her smile that made him glad not to look toward the doctor.

"I'll be getting on," said Channing.

"You can't go," she said. "Not till I've thanked you for the thing you've done for Larry."

The face of Channing stiffened. "That's unnecessary cruelty, isn't it?" he asked.

"Parker, be honest," she said. "It was all a game with you. You never cared a whit about me. I was simply a girl to fill some of the dull hours. Isn't that the truth?"

He stared at her. "All right," he said. "We'd better let it rest that way." Then he added: "No decent girl wants to think that a . . . murderer . . . ever cared for her."

"You're being serious?" she asked.

"My God," he exclaimed bitterly, "even if there's no heart in you, there ought to be a memory!"

"There is a memory," she answered. "You meant everything? Did you really mean everything, Parker?"

"There's no good in talking about it," said Channing. "I know what I'm going to do. I've seen what you think of me now. But so far as meaning what I've said before . . . well, I meant more than that, even when my damned supercilious manner denied my words."

After this, there was a pause that alarmed Traynor. He began to look anxiously from one to the other. And when he saw her beauty and the magnificence of the doctor, he could not help feeling that in some way they had been made, destined, for one another.

Then she said: "I'm sorry, Parker."

"You mean that," he answered very slowly. "And I'm such a poor beggar now that I'm grateful for even pity. Or is your blood still running cold when you look at me?"

"No," she said, shaking her head. "Only . . . it's the horrible waste, Parker. It's the frightful throwing away of all your chances . . . it's the ending of your life that makes me want to cry."

"Maudlin sentimentality," he answered, half sneering. "I'm ashamed of you, Rose. That's the weak streak appearing. I'll find my way to a new place in the world soon. Our friend Traynor thinks that he'll be able to find me on the out trail and stop me. For his own sake, I hope that he doesn't reach me . . . ever." And once more there was murder in the glance he gave Traynor.

A hunger suddenly came up in the heart of Larry Traynor, a burning desire for the future day when he would be able to confront the doctor clad in his full strength, without that deadly betrayal, that horrible fluttering of his heart and nerves.

"I'll go now," said the doctor.

"You can't go," said the girl. "You can't leave me alone with Larry. And I can't leave him here in danger."

"Danger?" echoed the doctor.

"Of course. The Whartons may swoop on the place at any time. And they . . . ."

"The Whartons are in prison!" exclaimed the doctor.

"They were in prison. Haven't you heard . . . but of course not. They broke jail. They . . . and a dozen other men. They started away through the mountains. They've been sighted here and there, close to this place."

"Ah," said the doctor, "and that's why your father moved off the ranch with the cattle?"

"That's right. The instant he knew that the Whartons were free, he was sure that they'd come straight for the ranch. He knew that they'd run off the cattle and burn the buildings. So he started for town."

"Why couldn't he have brought out a posse from town?"

"Hire thirty men for heaven knows how long? At five dollars a day and keep? Dad would rather die than throw away money like that."

"Rose," said Traynor, "do you mean that the Whartons at any moment may come down on the place?"

"It's true. They were sighted two days ago in Tomlinson's Gulch."

"Then what made you come out here . . . at night . . . into danger?"

"I'm ashamed to tell you," said the girl, blushing. "Well, I don't care . . . I'll show you."

She ran from the room. Her footfall went lightly down the hall, and Traynor smiled, listening after it, until his absent-minded glance crossed the burning eyes of the doctor.

"Some way . . ." said the doctor. He did not need to complete that tight-lipped sentence. *Some way* he would manage to cross and blast the happiness that she was dawning again for Larry Traynor. The cold white devil in his face glared steadily out at Traynor.

The girl came back. In her hand she held up a rose-colored frock, covered with airy flounces, the square-cut neck bordered with a film of lace.

"My first party dress," she said. "I looked through the luggage that my father brought in. When I couldn't find it, I made up my mind that I'd take this trip. I couldn't risk the lives of men by asking them to come along. So I told father that I was going to spend the night with Martha Carey . . . and then I came out here. I could be back long before the morning."

No matter what enmity was between them, the two men looked at one another and smiled. She, lowering the dress, suddenly cried out in a stifled voice of fear. Traynor followed the glance, and at the window, pressed so close to the pane that the nose and chin were whitened, he saw a man's face, rounded out like an owl's with an uncropped growth of beard, a man with eyes narrowed in malice. And the upper lip curled back from the teeth as though the man were a carnivorous creature, a hunting beast of the night. The face receded, sank out of sight like a stone wavering down into the dark depths of a pool.

"It's Jim Wharton!" gasped the girl. She slid down on her knees. "Oh, God, it's Jim . . . and all the rest will be with him!"

VII

The doctor got to the window with a leap, catching up the rifle on the way. He pulled up the sash and thrust the rifle out. A bullet smashed through the glass. Thudded into the opposite wall. The doctor stepped back into the corner, while loosed bits of the glass were falling with a tinkle to the floor.

Traynor, half dressed under the blankets, threw back the covers and began to pull on the rest of his clothes. He had shaped some heavy felt moccasins that he stepped into now.

"We've got to get Larry out!" the girl was crying. "He can't take care of himself now. Parker, we've got to get Larry out!"

"Do we?" said the doctor calmly. "We'll be in luck if we get anyone out."

He walked from the room and down the hall. Traynor followed. He was weak in the knees, and his head was light, but the gashes in his legs were fairly healed. He would have strength for short efforts, he felt sure.

They stood in the kitchen. The lamp had burned low and crookedly. It was smoking fast, and the sickening sweet smell of the soot hung in the air.

The doctor took control. "I'm going to try the back door, quietly," he said. "It may be that they haven't scattered all around the house yet. If I get out, the rest of you sneak after me. Keep on the left. We'll try to get to the shrubs."

Traynor had neared the door. It was perfectly apparent to him that the doctor was willing to take the risks. But there was a good reason why he should not.

Through the screen on the door, Traynor could see the pale glimmer of thin moonlight, pouring a haze of brilliance over the ground. He could see the gleam of strands of new wire along the corral fence. The barns were bleak and half white, half black shadow. The scene had the very look of death.

The doctor was still speaking when Traynor pushed the door soundlessly open and stepped out onto the porch. He had not taken two steps when he heard the stifled exclamation of the girl, behind him, and the doctor muttering: "Come back, you fool."

Then, out of the cloudy dark of a bank of shrubs behind the house, a thin tongue of flame darted. The crack of the rifle struck painfully against his ears. A sting greater than that of a giant hornet gashed his neck. He jerked the door shut as a second bullet hissed beside his ear as he side-stepped.

"They're behind the house . . . they're all around the house, it seems," said Traynor.

The girl parted her lips to speak, but no words came. She stood in white suspense while the doctor grabbed Traynor by the shoulders.

"You jackass," snarled the doctor. "This thing . . . thank God, is only a scratch." He pulled out a handkerchief and bound up Traynor's neck.

"Why did you do it, Larry?" begged the girl. "Why, why did you go out there, half helpless?"

"It's glory that the fool wants. Glory," sneered the doctor.

"Mind you," said Traynor, "I'll be no good to the rest of you. They're going to get me before the show's over, and they might as well get me now. You're the fool, Parker. You're the able-bodied man. It's up to you to get Rose away. You can't show yourself here and there to draw fire."

Channing, finishing the bandaging, stepped suddenly back at the end of this speech. The girl, with moisture welling into her eyes, stared mutely at Traynor.

"You see what he is," sneered the doctor. "A hero, eh? A dead hero before long, I suppose. We're all dead, Rose. And this is no time for damned heroics. Listen."

Outside, a man shouted. He was answered far and near, from all around the house, by what seemed a score of voices.

"We're walled in," said the doctor.

Traynor sat down and leaned his elbows on the edge of the table. He looked at the floor, forcing his eyes down because he did not want to let the image of Rose fill them. He tried to bend his mind away from the thought of her. As for what happened to him and the doctor, it was no tragedy. Men who live with guns in their hands have to fall by guns in the end, often enough. They were simply playing out their logical parts. But the girl . . . .

She stood beside him, now, resting a hand on his shoulder. The doctor paced the floor like a great cat. No one spoke. The nearness of the danger blinded their eyes and stopped thought.

Then a voice called: "Hello, you inside there!"

The doctor placed himself close to the door. "Hello, outside!" he answered.

"Who are you?"

"I'm Doctor Parker Channing."

"You're Doctor Murderer Channing, are you?" Sneering, drawling laughter commented on his name and presence. "Channing, you'd be better outside than inside. We could use a doctor like you. Open that door and walk out to our side of the fence and you'll be as safe as any of us."

Channing looked down at his hands and dusted them.

"Go on, Parker," urged the girl. "It's the best thing for you. You'll be safer with them than anywhere else. With them you may have a chance to get away."

"What do you suggest, Larry?" asked the hard voice of the doctor.

"You're a fool if you don't go out to them," said Traynor, peering into the pale face of Channing. "But I think you're going to be a fool."

"Do you?" asked the doctor with a slight start. "Thanks."

"Answer up, Doc!" shouted the man outside.

"Who are you?" called Channing.

"Jim Wharton."

"Wharton, I'm staying in the house with my friends."

A yell of amazement answered him. "Are you crazy, Channing? Are you gonna go home with your friends and let the sheriff hang you?"

"I'm staying here. That's final."

"Of all the damn' fools!" cried Wharton. And then, a moment later, he added: "There's another offer I'll make to you. Who's the second man in there . . . the one that was flat in bed?"

"He's Larry Traynor."

"Traynor? I got nothing against him. Now, listen . . . I've got men all around the house.

"I know that."

"Then you know that we can do what we please."

"I know that, too. But it might cost you something."

"Damn the cost. Or else, I can burn you out. And that's what I'll do if I have to!"

The doctor said nothing, but his head bowed a little and he took a great breath.

"But there's an easy way out of all of this," went on Jim Wharton. "It ain't everybody in the world that I'm against. It's the skunk that put me in jail. It's John Laymon that I'm going to get even with. Send out the girl to me. She's in there . . . I seen her myself."

"What sort of hound do you think I am?" asked the doctor.

"I think you got brains. I hope you have, anyway. We won't touch her. But we'll hold her till her old man pays for her, and pays heavy. Damn him, he's got enough money to pay. And I'm going to have a slice of it . . . a slice right into the red of it."

The doctor turned his head from the door toward Traynor and the girl. His eyes glazed. Traynor, starting to speak, found the hand of the girl over his mouth. The doctor seemed to see nothing.

"Answer up!" yelled Jim Wharton. "If you think that I'm going to wait an hour, you're loco. I get the girl, or else I burn out the three of you like rats!"

Suddenly the girl cried out sharply: "I'll come to you, Jim!"

"Good girl!" yelled Wharton. "You'll be safe with us, Rose!"

She had started up. The grip of Traynor fell on her wrist and checked her. "Let me go, Larry," she panted. "There's no other way for the two of you . . . ."

"They won't harm her," said the doctor. "They won't hurt her. She'll be safe, Larry, and . . . and . . . ." His voice faded.

"What he says is true!" cried Rose Laymon. "Larry, don't you see that?"

"Be still," said Traynor sternly. He jerked her down into a chair at his side. Then, his grim eyes never leaving the face of the doctor, he said: "You'd trust her with a gang of dogs like those fellows outside?"

"She'd be all right," insisted the doctor. "She'd be . . . I mean . . . fire, Larry! My God, if they set fire to this old wooden shack . . . the flames would . . . God! . . . they'd cook us."

"Are you coming, Rose?" shouted Jim Wharton.

"Be still," said Traynor.

"You damned fool!" shrieked the doctor, his voice shaking to pieces on the high note. "Do you want her to be burned to death?"

"Better that than the other thing," said Traynor. "Channing, what a skunk you are, after all."

"Rose!" called Wharton. "Where are you?"

And her eyes were bright and her voice was strong as she answered: "I'm not coming, Jim. I'm staying here!"

"Rose, if you stay there . . . woman or no woman, I'll fire the house. Do you hear?"

"I hear . . . and I'm staying!"

"It's crazy." The doctor gasped. "It's . . . fire, Rose! They'll burn the house upon our heads. They'll . . . ."

"Go out and argue with them," said Traynor sternly. "Maybe you can make them change their minds."

Parker Channing, leaning against the wall, struck a fist into his own face, and groaned. Then he muttered: "I'll talk to 'em face to face. I'm not afraid."

"I've given you your last chance!" yelled Jim Wharton. "Of all the damned . . . ."

"Wait a minute!" screamed the doctor. "I'm coming out . . . I'm coming out to talk to you! I'm going to . . . ." He opened the door. "Can I come safely?" he shouted again.

"Come ahead."

And Dr. Parker Channing slunk out of the house, without a word to those who remained behind. The outer door slammed, rebounded with a jangle, slammed again. And they knew that he would not come back.

"He's gone," whispered Rose Laymon. "Oh, Larry, for him to go . . . murder was nothing, compared to this."

A queer pain wrung the soul of Larry Traynor. "He's a brave man, though. I've seen him laugh at the idea of dying. Yes, with a gun leveled at him. But the fire, Rose . . . that's the thought that killed the heart in him. Never blame him again. The life that's in me, it's Parker that gave it back to me. He wouldn't be here now, except that he stayed to take care of me . . . ."

And a voice rolled in on them, faint from distance: "Throw the bush up there ag'in' the side of the house. Light that straw and throw it on, too!"

VIII

They could tell the course of the fire by the rising yells of the Wharton gang, then by the noise of the flames, and finally a tremor that went through the whole building. Beyond the window, they saw the smoke driving low in the wind toward the barns, which were wrapped in clouds, with the yellow light of the fire playing on it, until the barns in turn seemed to be on fire.

The two sat still for a long time. The wind carried gusts of heat to them over the floor. They could hear the far end of the building falling, as half-burned rafters crashed, and let down the roofs above them, and with every fall there was a louder roar of the fire.

Rose pressed closer and closer to Traynor. He, with his arm around her, looked steadfastly above her head. There was fear in him, but there was also a dim delight unlike anything he had ever known, a full and quiet ecstasy.

"Back there," she said, "if I could throw the months away . . . then I'd be happy, Larry."

"What months?" he asked.

"Those after I left you, and when I was knowing Parker."

"He is worth knowing."

"Do you mean that?"

"He is the greatest man I ever met," said Traynor solemnly.

"Larry, have you forgiven him out of the bottom of your heart?"

"I forgive him."

"Then I do, also."

"When the fire comes over the room, Rose, shall we make a break for the open?"

"No. Let's go with the house."

"There's the rifle with plenty of bullets in it."

She looked sharply up at him. "Well . . . that way, then," she murmured. Suddenly she cried out: "But I can save you, Larry! There's still time for me to save you, if I go out and call to them. They'll take me, and they won't harm me . . . ."

"Hush," said Traynor. She was still. He added: "I saw Jim Wharton's face at the window. Do you think I'd let you go out to him? It's better this way."

"It is better," she answered.

A strange light began to enter the room. The low-flowing smoke, wind-driven, covered the ground, and the fire reflected from the top of it through the window, brighter than the light of the lamp. This tremulous and rosy glow made the girl as beautiful as an angel to the eye of her lover.

As he looked at her, he said: "Poor Channing. Poor devil. He's out there thinking of this, Rose. He's eating his heart out. He's half wishing to be back in here with us."

"I don't want to think of him," she said.

"He killed poor old Sam. I ought to hate him. If we both lived, I suppose I'd try to go on the trail after him. But this way, I understand him. I'm glad to think of him. If it's God that makes us, He put too much mind and not enough heart in Channing. That's all there is to it. God help him, and God forgive him."

A voice shouted huskily, as if in fear: "Hey, all of you! Watch through that smoke! Watch through that smoke! They might sneak out that way, through the smoke!"

"And we might!" cried the girl. "Look, Larry!"

There was a great crash that shook the entire house—what was left of it. The walls of the kitchen leaned crookedly. Plaster fell in great chunks from the ceiling and seemed to drop noiselessly, so huge was the uproar of the fire, and the heat was intense. The flame could not be more than a room away. The door of the dining room rattled back and forth as though a hand were shaking the knob.

But out the window, Traynor could see hardly a thing. For the funnels of white smoke, rushing away from the house, filled the air and covered the ground, toward the barns.

"Rose," he said, "there's a ghost of a chance."

He went to the dining room door and pulled it open. Before him a wild furnace was roaring, tossing up a billion-footed dance of flames. The heat seared his face, searched his body through his clothes. He jammed the door shut again.

"Half a minute!" he called to the girl. "Have you got a hand-kerchief. Then wet it in that pitcher, and tie it over your mouth and nose. Like this. You see?"

He used the bloody handkerchief of the doctor, unknotting it from around his throat, for the same purpose. When he looked again, the girl was masked in white. She furled up the lower lip of the mask and threw her arms around him. And he, pushing the handkerchief high on his head, took what well might be his last clear view of her.

They only looked, desperately, with great eyes; they did not touch their lips together because each was striving, in divine despair, to see the face before them as it might be transfigured in another life. Then they drew down the wet masks again and went out the door onto the porch.

The full heat of the conflagration struck them at once. And the sweep of the wind hurried them into the boiling columns of the smoke. He had her hand in his.

"Close your eyes . . . I'll guide!" he called at her ear, and jumped with her from the edge of the porch.

He had a deep breath of pure air in his lungs. He ran forward straining his eyes through the smoke that burned them, until the breath was spent in his lungs. They were far from the house, by this time, and the dim outlines of the barns loomed dark before him.

He threw himself flat on the ground and dragged the girl down beside him. She was coughing and gasping. But there, close to the ground, it was possible to breathe and fill their lungs with better air, for the smoke kept rising.

Voices were still shouting: "Keep a watch! Keep a watch! What's passing there?" And distantly a rifle cracked. Three shots—at some smoky phantom, no doubt—and the firing ceased. But it was a good measure of the peril into which they were running.

"Now," he said at the ear of Rose Laymon, and helped her to rise.

His knees were very weak. Yet he could stagger again to a run that carried them on toward the barns. The door of one yawned open right before them. He had carried the rifle slung in his left hand; now he transferred it to the right, and, as he did so, he saw forms loom into the shadows of the doorway, peering into the smoke.

"Hey!" yelled one. The voice was a scream. "Here they come . . . here! Here!"

Traynor fired from the ready, straight into the breast of that big, bearded figure. He turned and jammed the muzzle of the rifle into the face of the second man, and the victim staggered backwards, screeching out something about his eyes, firing a revolver repeatedly at nothingness.

The girl and Traynor already were far down the empty aisle of the barn, with flickering lights from the burning house entering the place. Behind them, they heard a great crashing, a loud whistling of the triumphant wind, and a gust of heat and light streamed with a thousandfold brilliance into the shadows of the barn.

That was what enabled them to see half a dozen horses tethered to the manger near the rear door. The frightened beasts were rearing and stamping and pulling violently back on the tie ropes to escape.

Rose Laymon threw up her hands in helpless terror at that mill of great, tigerish bodies, as she heard the stamping of the hoofs and saw the frantic eyes of the horses rolling toward the distant fire.

But Traynor, with a knife, cut loose the first two horses. They looked no better than ordinary broncos, but ordinary broncos would have to do. They could not pick and choose. He hung onto the reins of a fiery little pinto as the girl swung into the saddle.

She had the rear door of the barn open the next moment, and Traynor was barely able to hook a leg over the cantle of the saddle before his horse flew like a stone through the doorway and into the open night.

"This way! This way!" a voice was screeching. "This way, everyone! Here they go . . . and on horses! Ride like hell! She's worth a hundred thousand to us. A thousand bucks to the gent that snags her first."

Traynor, righted himself with a vast effort in the saddle, then shot his horse in pursuit of the flying pinto, and he heard behind him the swift beginning of the pursuit, the rumble of hoofs growing louder and louder as man after man joined the chase.

IX

They went up the easy slope of a hill that was half white with the moon, half trembling with the glow from the fire. The house of John Laymon lay prone, but huge red and yellow ghosts rose above it, dancing, sometimes throwing up great arms that disappeared in the upper air.

There was plenty of light for shooting, and the Whartons used it. "Get that damned Traynor, and the gal will give up!" the familiar voice of Jim Wharton was thundering.

The result was an endless shower of bullets. Many of them flew wide. He only knew of their passing by the clicking of them through the branches of the trees or by their solid thudding into the trunks. But others clipped the air close about him, whining small with eagerness, each like a dog that misses its stroke and has to rush on past the quarry.

They rounded the hill. They entered a narrow shoot of a glade that carried them straight out into the road for Little Snake. To have that road under them seemed to insure freedom. He saw the head of the girl go up; he heard her crying: "We're going to make it, Larry! They're not going to catch us!"

But he, glancing back, still smiling, saw that half a dozen riders had forged ahead of the rest and were gaining steadily.

"Ride ahead!" he commanded Rose. "You're lighter than I am. The pinto's a flash. You'll get to help first."

She shook her head, waving her denial. And as he stared at her, the blood trickling again from the open wound in his neck, he realized that she would never leave him—not now—not hereafter.

There are fools, he thought, who doubt the future. Those are the men who have never gone through the fear of death with a friend, in the knowledge that an equal faith is on each side. But for such as have endured the crisis, there must be a promise of life thereafter. An eternity of faith poured over him as he watched her at his side and saw the tight pull she was keeping on the head of the pinto. She could flash away from him in an instant, but all the dangers in the world could never persuade her.

They rushed around a great loop of the road, and behind them the beating of hoofs was louder and louder. Then the voices rose in a sudden triumph that was like a song. He looked wildly behind him, and saw the waving arms in the moonlight and the brandished guns.

He could not understand, until he looked ahead again and saw a solitary rider, straight up in the saddle, rushing his horse down the slope to intercept their way.

Would he come on them in time?

It seemed almost an even race, but at the end, as the pinto and Traynor's mustang struggled up a slope in the way, it seemed that the horse of the stranger was losing speed. He did not attempt to shoot. Perhaps he was afraid of striking the girl with a bullet. And Traynor himself held his fire with the rifle.

A roar of angry surprise rose from the crowd of the leading pursuers. Then a twist of the way cut off everything from the view of Traynor. He was amazed to hear an outburst of rifle fire, with yells of high dismay scattered through the explosions.

The beat of hoofs died out. Still the voices clamored furiously, far away. Still the gunfire beat more rapidly.

But the pursuit had died at that spot. What had happened? Well, he could save his breath for the work of riding, for he was very, very tired. His legs shuddered against the side of his horse, and his back was bending.

Hours seemed to flow past him, and more hours. He passed into a sort of trance through which the quiet, cheerful voice of the girl cut into his consciousness, from time to time. She was riding the pinto close to his horse. She was supporting him. And then he saw the lights of Little Snake clustered ahead.

"Do you know what happened back there?" she asked him as she gave the horses their last halt before making the town.

"Where?" he asked, his mind very dim.

"The rider who came down the slope . . . didn't you know him, Larry?"

"Ah, the fellow who almost cut us off, and then his horse petered out, or his nerve failed him?"

"His horse didn't give out, and he had as much nerve as any man in the world."

"What do you mean, Rose,"

"It was Parker Channing. I knew him by his way in the saddle. I knew him by the wave of his hand when I looked back. And I saw him turning against the rest of them."

"The doctor? You mean that he cut in to help stop them? You mean . . .? Rose, I've got to go back to him . . . ."

"Hush, and be still," said the girl. "He died hours and hours ago. They've killed him, and gone on. But not till he let us get safely away."

"Die? For us?" cried Traynor.

"Yes, for us," she answered.

And he knew that it was true. His brain cleared of all weakness. He looked ahead at the twinkling lights of the town and the glimmering stars, and it seemed to Traynor that the glory of the heavens descended without a check and overspread this earth.

Back there at the head of the hill, the doctor had charged in earnest to cut off the retreat of the two, for he felt that he had abandoned all shame and all virtue forever, when he left them in the condemned house. There was nothing for him, now, but to race forward into crime and greater crime and welcome the darkness of the future.

And there was a savage earnestness in his riding as he considered how close the two rode together, Traynor beside the girl. He wanted to kill Traynor—not with guns but with his hands. When the last life bubbled up under the compressed tips of his fingers, then only would he be satisfied.

What was it that changed him? It was when he saw, quite clearly by the moonlight, how Rose Laymon was reining in her pinto until its neck bowed sharply; it was when he understood perfectly her will to live or die at the side of Traynor.

If his strength was in his mind rather than his heart, perhaps it was in the quiet perfection of his thinking that he saw how the two were blended together for a single destiny that should be far higher than to be trampled down by the ruffians of Jim Wharton. And it was clear thinking, also, that showed him what he must do. No one would know. His reputation would not be cleansed by the act, unless the girl, perhaps, had recognized him by his riding. But he had to face the Whartons and check their pursuit.

So, as he swung into the road at the crest of the shallow hill, he turned straight back toward the pursuers and pulled his rifle out of its holster. He took good aim. The very first shot jerked back the head of the foremost rider, and with upflung arms the man dropped backwards out of the saddle. The second brought a yell of agony.

The party split to this side and to that. With screaming curses the riders fled.

He could ride after the fugitive pair now. But that was not his plan. To his clear brain the future of this act was very plain. His life was cast away. He had thrown it away and made it forfeit with the bullet that killed old Sam. Perhaps he had returned a partial payment by the slaying of the ruffian, who lay yonder, twisted in the road. But there was still more to do—it was a long account.

He got his horse into a nest of rocks and made the animal lie down. By that time, the tail of the pursuit had come up, and warning yells of the Whartons made the other men take cover. They began to spread out to this side and to that. Bullets, now and then, whirred through his imperfect fortifications.

He kept a keen look-out. He saw a shadow crawling between two bushes, took careful aim, and fired. The man leaped with a yell that burned like a torch through the brain of the doctor. One bound, and the fellow was out of sight. But he would remember this night for the rest of his days.

Suddenly, on his right, four men charged right up the hill for him. They came from a distance of fifteen yards. He dropped— one, two—and the remaining pair dodged to the side and pitched out of view behind an outcrop of rock.

One of the remaining two lay still. The other, groaning, got to his hands and knees and started crawling away. The doctor let him crawl. Something in the tone of that groaning told him that the bullet wound was through the body, and if that were the case . . . .

In the meantime, the pair under the rock so close at hand would be a thorn in his flesh. He had to keep his attention at least half for them.

Still he watched until he saw a head and shoulders lift from beside the rock. He had to snatch up his own rifle quickly. He knew that his bullet struck the target. The head bobbed down like a weighted cork, but right through the shoulder and into the body of the doctor drove the answering slug.

That was his end, and he knew it. Calmly—because there was the clear mind in him to the end—he prepared for the last stroke. He could not manage the rifle very well with one arm. But he had a borrowed Wharton revolver. That was in his hand as he roused the horse and slipped into the saddle.

The instant his silhouette loomed, the rapid firing began. He spurred the mustang straight toward the flashes of the guns. And a glory came over the doctor, and enlarged his spirit and widened his throat. The shout that came from him was like a single note from a great song.

So, firing steadily, aiming his shots, he drove his charge home against the enemy until a bullet, mercifully straight, struck the consciousness from him, and loosed the life from his body, and sent the unharmed spirit winging on its way.

* * * * *

They gave Parker Channing a church funeral. And the town of Little Snake followed him to the grave.

There was a very odd picture of Rose Laymon kneeling at the edge of the grave, dropping roses into it. The rest of the people held back. They knew it was her right, her duty, to play the part of chief mourner. And not a soul in Little Snake doubted that her tears were real.

Those who watched kept shifting their looks from the girl to the pale-faced solemn young man who stood not far behind her, with his head bowed. He was waiting for the end of the ceremony. He was waiting for Rose Laymon.

And it is fair to say that in all of Little Snake there was not a man who did not judge that Larry Traynor had come fairly by his happiness.

White-Water Sam

Frederick Faust saw thirty-seven of his stories—twenty-three of which were short novels and the remainder serials—published in 1932. All but two of the serials appeared in Street & Smith's *Western Story Magazine*. Nonetheless, that year saw the beginning of the end of Faust's almost exclusive relationship with *Western Story Magazine* when his rate was lowered from 5¢ to 3¢ per word by Street & Smith. "White-Water Sam", a first-person narrative about river boating in Alaska, appeared in the January 30th issue that year under Faust's George Henry Morland byline.

I

This happened after the White Pass Railway went through. I was out of a job because I had been working on the *Thomas Drayton*, and after the railroad was completed, of course, there was no more for that ship. A ship she was, too, and not just a dirty shake-down of a scow with an engine dumped into her, like most of the river craft. I don't suppose that any river boats were ever built for beauty, but the *Thomas Drayton* looked mighty handsome to me. She was as limber as a sword blade from crawling over sand banks, and she was as strong as a sword, too, for bashing a way through ice. At that time, what with her two funnels and her big, powerful engines, she was the finest thing floating in Alaskan waters.

I'll tell you how well she was finished off. She had steel sheathing over the blades of her paddles. Why? Well, so that in case of need you could back her through shallows at a sand bank and she would claw her way over like a dog, scrambling to pull a sled through soft snow. I loved that boat. She answered her helm like a bird dog, and there was nothing finer in the world, to my way of thinking, than the way she would tremble all over, from head to heel, when she went away under full steam. There was zest in her. She seemed to have a personal interest in getting where she ought to go.

But there she was now, tied up to the dock, as useless a thing as you ever saw. The wind was coming straight across the lake, knocking up some waves, and they rocked her a trifle from side to side and kept her image shuddering, deep in the water.

She had cost $40,000 or $50,000 if she had cost a penny; and now she was worth—well, perhaps there was a $1,000 worth of junk in her, if anyone cared to wreck her for what could be got out of her hide and bones, but nobody cared.

Not even Thomas Drayton cared. He'd made a couple of fortunes out of her, young as she was, and now he was only lingering long enough to collect a few debts that were owing to him, before he went back to his own country to live a life of ease.

Nobody cared about her except me, Joe Palmer. And what was I to her? Why, I was an ex-deck hand.

But the *Thomas Drayton* is only a part of this narrative. Another part, just then, was paddling the edge of the lake in a birch-bark canoe, a regular, trim-built Indian craft. I admired the way the fellow in the canoe was paddling, because, Indian style, he never took the blade out of the water entirely, but worked it back and forth with a sinuous movement, like a snake in the water. A fellow who is a master of a paddle, like that, is driving his canoe ahead, steadying her and steering her every instant with one and the same stroke. I got up from the tarry barrel I was sitting on to watch the stranger beach his boat, and then I saw that he was not a stranger at all.

Who he was, I couldn't spot, just yet. So many thousands of faces had passed across my vision while I was working on the *Thomas Drayton*, that my mind was a blur, but I knew that I had seen that big thick pair of shoulders before and had noticed something both lazy and powerful in the way they were used. Well, shoulders, if you take a good look at 'em, express character as much as the face.

Now, as he beached the canoe, I began to see something familiar about the face, too. For one thing, it was clean-shaven, and it was almost a shock to see anybody come to the landing, that far north, without a shadow of beard all over the face. Yes, it was a clean-shaven face, and a very ruddy, brown skin—the complexion I recognized, also. But the next moment, when a white bull terrier jumped out of the bow of the boat and climbed in front of his master up to the level of the dock, I knew my man.

I might forget the master, but I'd never forget that dog. Neither would you, if you could see him—fifty-five or sixty pounds of dynamite all fitted snugly under a glove of white velvet. He shone like marble, as he came waltzing along before his boss.

"Hello, Larry!" I called out.

I laughed as I said it, for I saw the man stop, in the same half-indifferent, half-smiling, half-pleased, and half-bored way, and wave a hand at me.

"Hello, Joe," he said.

I was surprised that he remembered me. But he was the sort of fellow who was always coming up with a surprise. That was one of the pleasant things about him.

He came over and shook hands with me. I looked him up and down, but he only looked me straight in the eye; yet, like a boxer, I knew that he was seeing every bit of me. He was smiling.

"What are you doing 'way up here, Joe?" he asked.

"I'm being an ex-deck hand," I said, "and I don't like the job, either. What about yourself?"

"I'm looking for a fortune," he said.

I laughed at that, as though everybody in Alaska were not doing the same thing.

"That puts you in a class by yourself, Larry," I said. "Hardly anybody else up here is after gold."

"It's different, Joe," he said. "You know, I'm tired of bumming around. I'm going to settle down now. I don't want much. They can keep their millions. I only want about a hundred thousand, working at interest. That's all. And a quiet life."

I laughed again. He kept on smiling, but I could see, or thought I could see, that he was more than half serious.

"What are you going to do?" I said. "Go out and dig it out of the ground?"

He shook his head. "I never believed in manual labor, Joe," he said. "It's hard on the back, and it dulls the wits. No, I won't do any digging."

"You've got to dig a little," I said, "even if you go prospecting."

"Do you?" said Larry Decatur. "Then I won't go prospecting."

"Oh, won't you?" I said.

"No," he said, "I won't."

There was a deal of finality about him. And I don't know why what he said didn't seem to me more absurd. But there was about him a certain quality that makes a man succeed in what he wants to do. The trouble with Larry Decatur, Laughing Larry, as a lot of people called him, was that he had never wanted to do very much. He was contented to sit a great deal of the time in the sun and let the world go by him. He was a sort of a tramp, not the kind that goes mooching around, you know, but the fellow who stumbles onto a packet of money here and a run of faro luck there. He is always getting flush, and then dropping everything little by little, never caring about what happens tomorrow.

Have you ever taken a cat by the four feet and held it upside down with the ridge of its back six inches from the floor?

Try it. When you let go of the cat, although it has only a hundredth part of the second to turn in, and it's thin air that it's twisting in, that cat will manage to wriggle over, and what hits the floor is not the backbone, but the four padded feet.

Well, Laughing Larry was that sort of a fellow. You could hold him in any position and, no matter how far you dropped him, he'd land on his feet. That was why I took his casual lingo, rather seriously, up there on the shore of Lake Bennett. There were always possibilities of serious meanings under his jesting.

"If you pass up the gold-digging business," I said, "I don't know where you'll start."

"I'm a capitalist," he said. "I'm just looking for the proper place to invest my money."

"Have you got a big wad?" I asked.

"The roulette was pretty kind to me, one day several weeks back," answered Laughing Larry. "So when I counted over my spuds and saw that I had a couple of thousand, I thought that I might as well invest the coin, instead of sitting down to spend it. It cost me five hundred, one way or another, to get up here, and I've got fifteen hundred left."

I laughed in dead earnest this time.

"Why, man," I said, "what are you talking about? The only thing that's cheap in Alaska is money. Fellows make fifty thousand one day and spend it the next. They'd pay fifty thousand for an idea, maybe. And you've got fifteen hundred?"

I laughed again.

The bull terrier growled up at me, softly as a purring cat.

"Stop it, Doc," said Larry Decatur. "This is a friend of mine. He doesn't like you, brother. But I'll fix that. Give me your hand."

He took my hand and brought it down on the head of Doc. The dog blinked, sniffed at my hand, and then lay down at his master's feet.

"Is that the same one you had down there in Phoenix, six years ago?" I said.

"Oh, was that where I knew you?" answered Larry Decatur. "No, this is the grandson of that dog. They come and go pretty fast, bull terriers do. They have a way of stepping into hot water and staying in it too long. But this one I've trained carefully, since he was a puppy. Doc stands for Docile. That's his real name. And docile he is. At least, he is to me. And that's what counts. He obeys me as far as he can hear me, and he's almost as useful to me as a valet. Yes, a valet with a gun that he knows how to use."

"He'll fight men, will he?" I said.

"He'll fight men," said Larry, with pleasure in his eyes as he glanced down at the dog, "and he'll fight dogs . . . he'll take a horse by the nose and hold him for you. He'll also throw a bull. He's an educated dog, brother, and only two years old. When I think how much more he knows than a two-year-old child, for instance, I wonder where we get this stuff about the superiority of humans. Docile, here, knows how to fight a man with a club, or a man with a knife, or a man with a gun."

"How does he fight a man with a club?" I said.

"Waits till he hits, and then goes in for him, for the club hand."

"And a knife?" I said.

"That's different. He jumps in with a couple of feints, and then he jumps straight for the knife."

"That would cut him up a good deal, wouldn't it?" I suggested.

"No, not much. That skull of his is close to the skin, and it's all casehardened steel. He gets a slit across the skull, and the next moment he has the hand of the knife artist in that long fighting jaw of his. Look at that jaw, will you!"

I looked. One look was enough. "And when it comes to a gun?" I said.

"He dodges and runs for it," said my friend. "But then he comes shifting back in and jumps from behind. The nape of the neck is his objective, when he jumps at a man with a gun."

"D'you mean to say," I said, "that he's ever taken a man by the nape of the neck?"

"Mostly only the dummies that I've trained him on," said Laughing Larry, "but there was a fool of a Portugee that had a big Dane, and, a few weeks back, the great Dane tried to eat Docile and was strangled while eating, so to speak. The Portugee came out to shoot Doc, and I told Doc to go for him. It wasn't pretty, but the Portugee was a bad actor and a gunman. It didn't break the fellow's neck, because his neck was too thick. But it was a terrible shock to his nervous system, and I don't think that he'll ever pull a gun again, not on man or dog. Joe, isn't it time for me to buy you a drink? And isn't that a saloon over there?"

I nodded and walked across the dock with him toward Bridgeman's place.

On the way, I said: "Don't be surprised if you see a girl shelling out the liquor behind the bar, because that's White-Water Sam's place."

"Who's White-Water Sam?" he said.

"Don't you know?" I said. "He's the fellow who tried like a crazy fool to run a paddle steamer through Miles Cañon. He got off the center of the boat, and the steamer wedged crosswise, and the current smashed it in two. Five men drowned, in that party, and only White-Water was pulled out by luck and a long rope. He's never been the same since. He lost his nerve . . . and he's a little batty. But there was a time when he was the greatest pilot in Alaska. His girl runs the bar, most of the time."

II

There were a dozen men in front of the bar. Big Ed Graem was the chief center of attraction. He always was, wherever he showed up. I supposed, when I was inside, that everybody in the world knew about Ed and his dog teams, his gold strikes, and the fortunes that he was always making and losing. But I've discovered, on trips to the outside, that the world doesn't know much about Alaska, after all.

Ed Graem was as big as a mountain, hard and heavy. He was as strong as the Yukon when it sends the spring flood smashing out to the sea, with a hundred million tons of ice groaning and leaping and heaping on it. He was wild enough to be at home in the wilderness of Alaska, and that's as wild as any man can well be.

He was absolutely honest; he was square and faithful to his friends; he never refused money to people who were down and out. He had been down and out himself enough times to know all about how it felt.

Of course, he had faults. He gambled away hundreds of thousands, literally, but in Alaska, in those days, we never considered gambling a fault. Money had to run wild in that country; it had to flow, as blood flows in the body. The real fault and the worst fault of big Ed Graem—Big Ed was what we mostly called him— was that he had a temper that was hung like a hair-trigger. He was always flying into a passion, and, when he was hot, he was sure to get into a fight.

He'd forget that he stood six feet four inches and weighed two hundred and forty pounds. I don't mean to say that he'd pitch into little fellows. No, but he'd charge a whole crowd of small fry and beat them up. There's the story of how he cleaned out a barroom in Circle City, in the old days, by picking up a Swede by the heels and using his body as a club. He cleaned out the bar that day, and the Swede was laid up for a year.

Big Ed pensioned him, and that was all right. But you couldn't blame men for being a little nervous when Graem was around. Ed in a barroom was like a stick of dynamite in a fire. He might simply make everything brighter and ten times warmer than before. Also, he might explode at almost any moment. But the fellows who stood in real danger were not the little chaps. It was the big ones who were liable to have a bad time.

You see, he seemed to go blind, and anybody, reaching up one to three inches over six feet, looked to Ed Graem like a fair match. I was around six-three myself, and I'd saved my own scalp from him twice by being able to run faster than that demon behind me.

The next day he always apologized and did his best to patch up the damage he had done. Although you may be able to salve a man's broken skin, it's hard to salve his broken pride. That's why there were scores of men in Alaska, in those days, who admitted all of Big Ed's good qualities, but who nevertheless hated him.

I thought of these things, as I took Larry into the barroom. And I couldn't help noticing that he was hardly more than an inch shorter than the giant, and within some thirty pounds of the weight of Graem, too. But I flattered myself that everything would be all right, because there, behind the bar, just as I had expected, stood Nelly Bridgeman, serving out the drinks.

She was rather a damper on the natural flow of conversation. Some fellows, who were used to swearing with every other breath after living in mining camps for years, were simply tongue-tied when she was around. But I've known fellows to travel two hundred miles just for the sake of sunning themselves for a couple of days in Nelly's presence.

She was no beauty, either. She was just a pretty girl, rather on the big side, with sandy-colored hair and gentle green eyes. She had a placid way of moving and speaking; her voice went easily into your ears, and the thought of it stayed in your mind for a long spell. She was simple-hearted and good. She was so simple that, on my word, I don't think she realized that whiskey is likely to addle the brains of a man. As a matter of fact, she never had much chance to see the effects of it, even when she was serving behind the bar, because the moment anyone got glassy-eyed or began roaring, two or three of the boys would be sure to lead him outside, where he could cool off.

But the chief reason that I was glad to see her behind the bar on this day was that I knew Ed Graem was crazy about her. He'd been trying to marry her for a year, and the only reason he didn't succeed, we all believed, was because she didn't want to saddle her father on any other family until his wits were less addled. Until he came through his mental sickness, therefore, she was there to care of him. No one else could do the job.

I depended upon Nelly to keep the atmosphere calm. I was the only man, besides Larry, that stood tall, and Ed had seen me around enough—chased me around enough, you might almost say—to know me and be friendly even when he was in one of his wild tempers. Yes, Ed would know me. But he did not know Larry.

I wonder if it's right for me to say, also, that I wasn't altogether without a sort of curiosity, wondering if big Larry could run fast enough to get away from Big Ed.

Some of the others in the barroom were curious, too, as I could see from their grins. Particularly, there was that rascal of a Thomas Drayton, my old boss, standing in a corner of the bar and grinning from ear to ear, as he looked Larry up and down.

It wasn't the men who started the trouble, though. It was the dog. Right at the heels of Big Ed sat his newest and best leader, a hundred-and-fifty-pound brute of a MacKenzie Husky. And already that dog was rolling its red eyes toward Docile.

Well, I paid no great attention to that, as I edged into the bar and waved to Nelly Bridgeman.

She came down at once, leaving Big Ed leaning with his elbows on the bar, like a falling tower. I introduced her to Larry, and she shook hands and gave him a smile. She said that she was always very glad to meet any friends of Uncle Joe.

It irritated me a good deal to be called that. I was about forty, in those days, and I really felt that I was hardly entering middle age. No man is ready to be called middle-aged until he's made some sort of a position for himself. Joe Palmer, ex-deck hand, wanted some other title before being referred to as Uncle Joe.

That scoundrel of a Larry Decatur saw how I felt, too, and he was chuckling as the girl gave us our drinks, collected the money, and went back to continue her chat with Big Ed. But even that short interruption had been enough to put him on edge, and started him glowering up the line toward Larry.

Larry didn't notice it.

He turned to me and said: "You're not as old as you seem to twenty. I suppose she's twenty, eh?"

"I suppose so," I growled, still feeling a bit hurt, and herded out of things.

"She'd make somebody a wife," he said. "She has the look of a wife in the making."

"Ed Graem's going to marry her, I suppose," I grunted.

Larry turned and surveyed the situation.

"That fellow?" he said. "He's a mountain, not a man."

"He's got half a million or so, for the tenth time," I said. "That's Big Ed Graem. He's famous all over the country."

What Larry said next surprised me.

"It's easy to get famous," he answered. "He's got too much muscle to have much brain. By the time his blood's through nourishing that hulk, there's nothing left to feed his gray matter."

"Isn't there?" I asked. "You'd better not let him hear you say that, though. His temper is as short as his body's long. And he's likely to tie you in knots."

"No, he won't tie me in knots," answered Larry.

I looked sharply up at him, and he repeated: "He won't tie me knots. It takes a clever fellow, with a lot of luck, to tie me in knots. Just so many pounds of Percheron won't turn the trick."

He said this not half as softly as he ought to have said it. And little red-headed Mickey Callahan, standing next to us, gave a long, hard look at my companion.

I didn't like that look. Mickey was the sort of a boy who would talk free, wide, and handsome. And a couple of words in the ear of Graem might be enough to wreck the whole place,

I was glad to hear the voice of Tom Drayton, saying pretty loudly at the far end of the bar: "What good is she to me now? Nothing to run her for on Lake Bennett, any longer, and there's no way of getting her down into the river without running Miles Cañon and the rest of it. That can't be done. I'd give her away for a thousand dollars."

Then Larry lifted his head.

"I have a thousand dollars, stranger," he said.

III

That was an odd remark, considering that we were in Alaska. It was not odd in my ears, because I knew something of the nature of Larry Decatur, but the others did not know him. They laughed and then they whooped.

The grin widened still more on the face of Tom Drayton.

"If you got as much as a thousand bucks, you're a lucky boy," he said.

Everyone laughed some more. Big Ed Graem turned his head, brooding on Larry, and the sound of his jeering laughter cut through the rest of the noise and zoomed above it. He could be an irritating fellow all right. He looked to me, just then, like a cross between a wolf and a bear. There was a look in his eyes that I had seen there before, and I didn't like it.

"What's the her that you'll sell for a thousand dollars?" asked Larry perfectly calm in the midst of the laugher, and smiling himself, and at ease.

I couldn't help admiring his attitude. I couldn't help wondering, too, if his brains had not deserted him for once in his life.

"The her," said Drayton, "is the *Thomas Drayton*."

He laughed again as he said this, and everyone else laughed. There was a mob feeling in the air, and that mob wanted to make a fool of Larry. Therefore, a fool he had to be in spite of the facts.

I said at Larry's ear: "Let's get out of here. There's trouble in the air."

"Sure, there's trouble," said Larry Decatur. "That's why I'm going to stay. I like trouble. I haven't had a good dish of it for months."

In the face of all their laughter, he laughed a bit himself.

"If she is named the *Thomas Drayton*," said Larry, "she sounds more and more interesting. What can she do?"

"She?" answered Drayton. "Oh, she can swim white water, and she will swim it for her boss. She never says no, and she works like a demon, day and night. She's big and she's kind, take it from me."

"She sounds better and better, this *Thomas Drayton*," said Larry. "Is she a dog?"

How they howled with laughter as he said this.

I barked at him: "She's a big river boat, lying out there on the lake. Don't be a fool!"

He merely winked at me. "I'll take her for the thousand," he said.

"I'll shake with you on that and have the money," said Drayton. "It'll take me home, safe and sound. In comfort, too, without spending any capital . . . and you can stay here and live comfortable with the *Thomas Drayton*."

Everyone whooped and howled again. Then, as Drayton came striding up, I heard the sneering, snarling voice of Ed Graem saying something about born fools never getting any sense, no matter how long they lived.

Larry took that, and pretended not to hear it. No one was surprised that he took it. It was the fashion to take things from Ed Graem, just as if he were a madman.

Another voice cut in, cool and unhurried. It was the girl, Nelly Bridgeman, who was saying: "You won't cheat a stranger, Tom, will you? You'll let him know that the big boat's of no use, won't you?"

There was a lot of concern in her gentle face and those kindly, big, green eyes.

Tom Drayton was irritated, rather naturally, to be interrupted in the midst of a good bargain. And a good bargain it was for him. I don't suppose that there was another man in the Northwest who would have paid down a penny for the *Thomas Drayton*, fine boat that she was.

He was taking a sheaf of greenbacks from the willing hands of Larry and shaking hands on the bargain at the same time, while he barked over his shoulder at the girl: "And why ain't the *Thomas Drayton* worth something? All that's gotta be done with her is to run her through the rapids, and she'll be out on the lower river, where she'll be worth a hundred thousand, I'd say, at this season, with half a dozen new strikes going on, and men willing to pay their weight in gold to get themselves taken to the new diggings. Why ain't she worth a measly thousand dollars? By Jiminy, I've got a mind to take her back myself. I would, too, except that I'm tired of the transport business. But don't you go horning into a man's business affairs, Nelly!"

"Shut up, Tom," said half a dozen voices all at once. "Shut up and back down. You know who you're talking to?"

He did know, too, and he turned a bright red, realized that he had made a fool of himself. Afterward, he went as pale as he had been red, for he saw the giant form of Big Ed Graem towering above him.

There might have been trouble here, again; the air was becoming surcharged, when an unexpected voice broke in. The instant it began, it stopped all other talk.

"And why not run a steamer through Miles Cañon and the rest? Why not?"

It was Bridgeman, poor old White-Water Sam, standing there behind the bar, long and lean, with his bent shoulders and his starved, hollow chest. His hair was silver—pale, untarnished silver—but over his eyes the brows remained as black as jet. They, and a peculiar way he had of looking down and smiling, gave him a diabolical look, although we all knew that there was no evil in old Sam. It was simply that he had been too deep and too long in torment.

He was looking down in the old way now, smiling and nodding his head a little.

I knew what was likely to come; so did everyone. So, most of all, did poor Nelly. She gave a wild look around for help, and then she went to her father, put her hand on his arm and looked up at him with such gentleness, pity, and fear for him, that I wondered how even a man who was two thirds mad could meet that look without being braced up a little by it.

She said: "Daddy, I wish that you'd get some wood up for the stove, will you? I've got to have a hot fire for baking bread, you know, and . . . ."

"Why, Nelly darling," says Bridgeman, "I've got the place heapin' with wood. Don't you worry about there being enough to bake the bread. There's wood heaped around like there was wood heaped on the *Denver Belle*, that time that she ran Miles Cañon."

He laughed. Nelly drew away from him, as though knowing that nothing could stop him, now that he had started. I felt sick, and, glancing about me, I saw that the others in the room looked white and strained, too. A couple of fellows went sidling out through the door. But the rest of us all stayed to face the music, not because we wanted to listen, but because at the end of that story there was always the mischief to pay, and we wanted to stand by and help Nelly.

I remember that Big Ed stood there by the bar with his head dropped and resting on one hand, while he set his jaw and endured until the end what had to be heard.

There was only Larry in the entire room, who did not seem moved. Of course, he could not tell the thing that was to come. He never had heard it.

Then old Sam Bridgeman went on: "You boys must have heard about the way the *Denver Belle* ran Miles Cañon? No?"

He seemed to take the silence in exactly the wrong way, as one of questioning excitement, and now he looked up with a happy laugh of exultation.

"Well, it's a pretty good story," he said. "You boys may've heard her name, even if you didn't hear her greatest voyage. The *Belle* wasn't much. She was a little one-stack scow, but she was worth money . . . and she'd be worth twenty times as much below the rapids as above it, as stands to reason. So, by thunder, they decided to run her through the chute. And the first thing that they wanted was a first-rate, bang-crack pilot, d'ye see? So they fetched around a compass, and they come on a pilot named White-Water . . . White-Water . . . let me see, what was the rest of his name? I disrecollect. Some of you boys may know. Eh? Well, I'm getting old, and the first sign is that I can't recollect nothing right."

I moistened my lips and took a breath. I wanted liquor badly. There was poor Sam, poor old White-Water Sam unable to remember his own name. But that was the way he always started that cursed story.

Nelly Bridgeman had turned away and was standing there with her head bowed, holding herself hard. And I could see the shudders run across her shoulders and all through her body, poor girl.

"Anyway," said Bridgeman, "this pilot I'm telling you about, he went and took a look at the *Denver Belle*, and he saw that she was a flimsy wreck, and, if ever she so much as touched the wall of Miles Cañon, either side, she was no better than done for. So whatcha think he done? He took and strung bales of hay all around her!"

As he said this, Bridgeman lifted his head once more and looked about triumphantly, as though to win applause for the hero of his story. He was so rapt that he failed to notice the sick, pale faces of the men who were listening to him. Oh, it was a bad moment for us.

"And then," said Bridgeman, "when he had the old boat ready, he got up plenty of steam in her. He had for a crew only five men that were old friends of his . . . that would've trusted old White-Water to the infernal regions and back. And he turned her loose, and he shot her into Miles Cañon, where the water was churned white as milk, and the force of it heaping the current high in the middle. Right on the middle of that ridge, like a circus rider on the back of a galloping hoss, that was where White-Water rode, because he had a touch on the wheel more delicater than the touch of a girl threadin' a needle."

As he spoke, he held out his hands before him, as though they grasped the wheel in the pilot house once more, and, as his head went back, the long white hair fell away from his face, and we could see the glory in it and the smile that must have always been there when he had fought his way through a thousand rushing cataracts.

"And White-Water felt the current take hold of the old *Denver Belle* like a hand takes hold of a stone, and then throws it, and he knew, if he let the prow slide a yard or two from the center of the piled-up ridge, the old boat was gone. But he knew that he wouldn't let it slide. He laughed in his heart, I tell you, and knew that he would bring the *Denver Belle* through with the five men that trusted him enough to follow him to Hades and back."

I had to take hold of something, and what I gripped was the arm of Larry. His face hadn't changed color and it still wore the faint, good-humored smile, but his arm was tense and as hard as a rock.

"Well," said Bridgeman, "White-Water balanced that old tub on the middle of the ridge of water like a man walking on the edges of swords and a chasm under him. And then . . . then . . . then . . . ."

His voice shot up into the note that we had all been waiting for, taut and hardened, and for that very reason it hit us all the harder and broke us, because we were brittle with the expectation. It was a sort of scream and a strangling, together, and the joy went out of his eyes and left a staring horror in them.

"She slipped! The prow slipped. A demon pushed it off the ridge, and the *Denver Belle* jammed straight across the channel, filling it, and the current bashed in the sides of her like a matchbox. As she went, I was screaming in the pilot house . . . 'Take me, and leave them five go free!'"

He got that far, when Nelly turned about, white but steady, and made a sign. I leaped over the bar with a fellow named Dan Winton, and we caught hold of old Bridgeman. But poor old White-Water Sam wasn't violent at all this time. He just wilted into our arms, and we got him out of the barroom and into his bedroom, and we stretched him out on the bed and left Nelly with him. She could handle him, now, and nobody half so well, as he lay there turning his poor, crazy face from side to side and saying over and over: "They followed me to torment, but I couldn't bring 'em back! I couldn't bring 'em back!"

The two of us, we soft-footed out of the room.

IV

As we turned at the door, I remember that Nelly Bridgeman was sitting on the bed close to her father, putting a hand on each side of his mad face and saying to him, over and over again, that it was only a dream he'd been having, and that there never had been a *Denver Belle*. Well, as I looked back at the pain and the courage in her face, I realized why all of us respected her so much.

Then we went out into the barroom.

I heard Big Ed roaring at Tom Drayton: "Who began all of this chattering about a boat, anyway? Who began talking about running a boat through Miles Cañon? You all know what that does to the old man."

Drayton was scared to death. He wasn't the size and he wasn't the age to be one of Graem's victims, but one never could tell when the giant would lose all control and get his horrible hands on a mere child, even.

It was no wonder to me that Drayton was scared, and I was amazed to hear Larry break in with: "I started talking about the boat, Graem."

Graem turned around and almost shouted with joy, when he saw a man of about his own size, if you can call thirty pounds' difference anything like an equality. He came striding over toward Larry Decatur, calling out: "I just wanted to know where the blame ought to be put! I'd rather put it on you, you . . . ."

Of course, the way he strode along was enough to scatter the crowd before him, and leave Larry naked to the wrath of Big Ed. That wrath had been gathered and stacked up, so that it was quite ready to break on the head of someone.

His anger was so apparent that the trained dog, Docile, slipped out before his master and lowered his head and growled, soft and low, after the way that bull terriers have. From the looks of 'em, the very moment they are ready to fight, they seem most ready to turn and run away.

That must have been what the great Mackenzie Husky thought, also. At any rate, he came rushing around the knees of his master and took a dive at the white dog, and Docile knew perfectly well that he needed room. At any rate, he whipped about and ducked through the door of the saloon into the street.

We all wedged our way out after him, and there we saw the Husky—what a magnificent brute that dog was!—cleaving the air and baring his teeth to get them into Docile.

He looked business, and business was what he meant, and business was what he knew. Docile ran to meet him, and then dropped to the ground and took a long, shallow slash down his back as the wolf dog sailed over him.

Docile reached up for the throat, but he only tore out a big mouthful of wool.

Then the terrier stood up. He spat out the fur and waited, blinking his eyes for the next rush.

"Stop! Stop it!" yelled somebody. "This is just murder."

"The white rat needs killing!" shouts Big Ed. "I'll use my hands on the gent that tries to interfere!"

That was enough to keep anyone from intervening. And the Husky, turning about, dived at the dog again. You know how a Husky fights? It's like a wolf—a flash of the teeth and a slash as he comes in, then an attempt to give his shoulder to the enemy and bowl him over on his back. Once that happens, the teeth can get freely at the throat, and one rip is enough to finish the fight. In a sense, it's fencing. The teeth are used as the sword. It's not a matter of taking hold and locking the teeth in a grip; it's rather a matter of cutting for the life and getting away again, before there can be a return stroke. Well, the Mackenzie came in like that.

I glanced over at big Larry Decatur, to see how he would take the murder of his dog, but I was surprised to notice that he was as cool as a cucumber. He merely yawned a little and shrugged his shoulders.

The Mackenzie, rushing in, tried the old dodge, a shoulder stroke and slash of the teeth combined. The terrier paid no attention to anything else. He was bleeding along the back, and he seemed to realize, after the first attempt, that it was useless to try to trip up a wind-footed creature like this. I suppose, many a time, he had tangled up big dogs and brought them down with that old device, but now he discarded it after a single trial and did a new thing. He played for the head.

That's the bull terrier instinct. They keep working at the head. Most of their own scars will be around the head, too, not so many on the body.

Now Docile played his teeth at the great, flashing fangs of the Husky, and there was a clash that sounded like metal on metal.

The Husky bounded away with nothing accomplished, and stood shaking his head, his tongue lolling. I don't suppose that he liked the feeling of the teeth that had clashed against his, but this was an old story with the bull terrier. He didn't shake his head. He just pricked his ears, wagged his snaky tail, and trotted in for more.

We yelled when we saw that.

"Your Husky's got a handful!" somebody bawled across at Ed Graem, but Ed merely sneered and tried to laugh.

There was the Husky jumping again in a fury, and again the clash of teeth, as the smooth, hard head of the terrier played straight for the teeth of the other.

The Mackenzie backed away in three long bounds, sat down on the ground, and howled.

It was a strange thing to see. We all laughed a little, although I don't think that any of us felt exactly like laughing. But it was odd to notice the way that wolfish demon, that had probably murdered twenty dogs in his time, took this failure of the age-old tactics.

Docile had brains, you see. He had brains, and he'd been trained to use them. The wilderness is a mysterious and a great thing, and the creatures in it know a lot. But suddenly I remembered what Larry Decatur had said not long before—that he was not afraid of anyone who didn't fight with brains.

The Husky was ready to stop and think a bit. But Doc was not for stopping. He just wagged his tail and dashed in again. The Mackenzie, with a roar, bristled, and they were off once more. This time the teeth met, but they did not part. As the dogs swung around, I thought that each of 'em had a cheek hold, locking them together.

Then I saw what had really happened. The upper part of Docile's muzzle was fairly between the jaw of the wolf!

It was a horrible thing to see. I remembered what a Husky could do with his jaws, and I half expected to see the upper jaw and the whole foreface of the terrier bitten away.

Then I noticed that it was the Husky that was backing away, and trying to tail off. Docile seemed as happy as could be.

Gradually, in the midst of the excited yelling of the men, I saw what had happened. I have said that Docile weighed fifty-five or sixty pounds, and now all of that weight was hanging onto the lower jaw of the Mackenzie.

There, his grip was locked, and on that lower jaw his own teeth were closing and grinding.

If the Husky tried to bite in turn, he had sixty wriggling and athletic pounds to lift before he could make an impression on the skull of the dog. And even the steel-trap muscles of a Husky's jaw will begin to give way, after a time. These were giving away, at any rate. They were failing. The mouth of the Mackenzie sagged open, and he was trying to get away, struggling with all his might, until he stumbled or tripped and fell flat on his back.

Docile let go, then. He let go and grabbed hold again, on the throat, exactly beneath the roots of the jaw. Such was his strength, as he fitted his teeth into a hold and shook his head, he lifted the whole ponderous body of the Husky.

The fight was over and the Husky as good as dead. He could only claw. His mouth gaped, and his tongue thrust out.

Then Larry Decatur stepped and said: "I guess that Husky has enough. Let him go, Docile."

You know what a dog is in the middle of a fight, especially a bull terrier or a bulldog. But I give you my word that the instant that white beast heard his master's voice, he let go and turned the big fellow loose.

It was almost startling.

The Husky, his throat streaming red, got up, staggering, hanging down his head, and Docile came back to his master, smiling as only a bull terrier can smile, and licking his chops.

V

Right here, I want to ask charity for Big Ed. You see, he'd had his way for years. No man ever had dared to cross him. If he were checked by a crowd, it was always the worse for the crowd.

Tonight, he had seen his girl upset, and attributed the trouble to Larry Decatur. Also, he had seen his favorite dog humbled, and a man can stand almost anything sooner than see his dog licked—such a dog, too, with brains and fighting talents, to be thrashed by a white rat!

At any rate, remember that Ed Graem had other qualities of the heart besides an impulse toward brutality and his own way. But now the good in him was down, and the bad was up with a vengeance.

He came with his great strides toward Larry, and the dog skulked at his heels, until it saw that the direction led toward the same mysterious brute that had almost sapped his life. Then he stopped and backed up.

I wish that Graem had backed up, too.

"Sorry your dog was hurt," said Larry Decatur, "but it seemed to want trouble."

"You've got a trained dog," said Big Ed, almost frothing. "You've got a vicious sneak of a poison-trained trick dog, and I dunno that you're any better than a dog yourself. You've done enough harm around here for one day. It's time you had a lesson."

"Lessons are what I'm always looking for," said Larry, as mild as you please. "Sometimes I give 'em, and sometimes I take 'em. How are you going to teach, brother? With a knife, or a gun, or your hands?"

Big Ed paused in his stride.

"A gunman!" he roared.

"Take this gat, Joe," said Larry, handing a revolver to me. He seemed to have picked it out of the air. "And now, I'm not a gunman, Mister Graem."

"I'm going to trim you down to a better size," said Graem, balling his fists.

"Now, between you and me," said Larry, "how much would you bet that you'll trim me?"

"I'll bet you, ten to one, if you wanna bet on your dirty hide," said Graem, trying to laugh, and only strangling himself.

"I always pick up the easiest kinds of money when they come my way," declared Larry. "I have five hundred here. Joe, hold this, too. I'm stacking up five hundred, Mister Graem. Let me see the color of your coin, will you?"

"My word's better than your money around here," said Graem, which was true enough. "Put up your hands, you hound!"

Then, speech failing him, he rushed in at Larry with both his hands out, ready to grab him.

He looked formidable enough, as he charged in, although anybody could have told that he was making a clumsy rush. But everything formidable about him was divided in half when Larry made a half step forward and slammed him with a beautiful, long, powerful straight left, right on the chin.

You know, there's this about a straight left, it's no knock-out punch, but it's like running into a wall. And Big Ed was running as hard as he could, when he met that lunge, and the spat of the fist against his face was like the clapping of your two hands together.

He stopped and went back on his heel.

Larry made a perfect shift—that is to say, he moved his right foot a whole step forward, and, as that foot hit the ground, his right fist cracked the side of Ed Graem's jaw with a thud five times harder than the first punch.

A shift is a clumsy punch and a hard one to land, but when it connects it generally brings home the bacon.

Stanley Ketchel, of unlucky memory, was the great artist with that wallop. He would walk in, using his feet and hands together, like a pacing horse, and the way he socked was something to write home about. He didn't care for size. The bigger the man, the more punching surface.

When Larry Decatur slammed Ed Graem with that right shift and nailed him on the button, we all saw a thing that had been looked for but never hoped for in the Arctic for years—Graem staggering back from a blow, with his hands hanging down.

We yelled, not exactly with pleasure, but in sheer astonishment, to see it happen. A couple of the fellows who had felt the weight of Graem's hands in other days, here and there, simply howled at the sky, like wolves.

"He's met his master!" screeched one of them.

I didn't believe that. No one could believe it, looking at the bulk and the iron-hardness of Graem and the soft-looking exterior of Larry Decatur. I knew that in the Southwest, Larry was considered a terrible fighting man, but I didn't know what his weapons might be.

However, the fight was not over, and I looked to see the next move of Graem not half so clumsy as the first. I was right. He got himself together with a shrug of the shoulders, shook the mist of darkness out of his head, and merely grunted: "Prize-ring stuff, eh? I'll show you how far that goes up here."

Then, in he came at Decatur again. Larry stood off with his hands on his hips, laughing a little. "I hate to collect five thousand dollars on this," he said. "This is too easy."

Then Graem came in with a bound and a roar. He'd heard that remark, and it simply maddened him. It put out his brain, like a shot between the eyes.

"I'll show you how to collect," he said.

He came in with the proper stance, this time, with a long left held out before him like a great beam, the right poised, ready for a punch—and any punch he landed was likely to be the finishing one, we all knew.

A frightful thing, it was to see so much manhood in such fast action, I can tell you. It made my heart cold, and yet it made my heart beat fast with a sort of crazy joy in the excitement of the thing.

I didn't see how Larry, or any other man, could get past that long, monstrous left, but he managed it in the way you would least expect. He simply ducked under and came up inside as fast and as light as a sparrow bobbing at a seed of grain.

When he was inside, he slammed Big Ed Graem half a dozen times, so fast you could hardly see them.

You could hear them, though. They thudded home like hammer strokes. You could see, moreover, the effect of 'em on Graem.

He was a mountain, all right, but even a mountain can be blasted off its base, if sufficient powder is used. He staggered, he reeled, and then he went back before that storm.

Only at the last, he flung out his left hand with a sort of desperate, defensive gesture, and happened to click Larry alongside the head.

I give you my word that it was almost an accidental punch, but, to show you the terrible power of that man, the mere glance of that casual blow knocked Larry into a whirl and a stagger. And there was Graem, standing back, shaking the mist out of his head, scowling, but ready to fight till he died.

We? Well, we were yelling our heads off.

Then I looked to Larry, and saw that he was badly hurt, indeed. There was on his face the strained look of a fellow about ready to cash in, and his knees were sagging. It was as though not a human hand, but a steel-shod beam had grazed his head.

But by thunder he cried out: "Come on, Graem! Come on, you man-eater, and let me show you up? Or do you want me to come for you, eh?"

Graem parted his lips for a snarl and, still snarling, he came in, smashing out furiously, but half blindly.

Larry ducked under the thrust of that blow, and, with a swinging overhand right, he turned the snarl of Graem into a crimson smear. It was a pretty punch and a terribly hard one. It put Graem back on his heels, and, while he was back there, Larry smashed both fists into the pit of his stomach.

Those blows would have killed most men. They would have torn out my heart for one. But from the whalebone and India rubber of Graem, they merely rebounded. He grunted once for each blow, and, rocking forward again from his heels, he whanged Larry on top of the head.

To hear the thud of those blows, you would have said that every one of Graem's knuckles had been driven halfway up the back of his hand, but nothing like that had happened, as a matter of fact.

His hand wasn't hurt at all, and Larry made a reeling step back and sank on one knee.

He was gone. He was done for, I knew.

But he had put in enough punishment to make Graem square off in the wrong direction, still shaking his head to get rid of the mental fog that would not disappear.

I heard some of the fellows, and it made me mad to hear them, screeching at Graem that he had his man, and to come on in and finish him off.

But what did Larry do? Well, waiting there on one knee, his face as white as death, he called out: "Hey, Graem? What's the matter? Why don't you make a fight out of it? Do I have to wait here sitting down all day for you, you big yellow-livered hound? You four-flushing quitter?"

A sort of moan of wildest rage choked the throat of Graem, and he came in with a rush that was totally blind. He could not see. Partly the blows he had received had addled his brain, and partly fury blinded him.

He came in, and Larry, rising, struck with the rise of his body and the spring of his legs, a long, updriving straight right, with all the weight of his body behind it.

I could see that; I could see it hit the button of the side of Graem's jaw, and I could see Graem's knees sag and his hands drop.

He was out on his feet.

Larry drew back, collected himself, poised his right, and stepped in to strike that blank and awful face.

Then he stopped himself, and turned away.

"Somebody give him a drink," he said. "He needs one, I think."

VI

I turned just then in time to see something that I wish that I had never seen—Nelly Bridgeman, as white as stone, at the door of the saloon. She must have seen the whole thing or, at least, she had seen the critical part of it.

Then I watched Graem being led away by a couple of the boys. He was still all out, his head rolling on his shoulders from the effects of that terrible last blow, but all the same his legs held him up, his legs that had mushed so many thousands of miles with racing dog teams.

They took him, the fools, straight toward the door of the saloon. When he got there, he saw the girl and suddenly the sight of her jerked him back to his full senses.

He realized what had happened. He realized that he'd been beaten in the presence of the girl he loved and in the presence of a crowd of gaping witnesses. And he threw up his hands and went staggering off into the woods.

Larry Decatur, breathing hard, his fists still clenched, looked after him. His own face was gray and drawn. He had been near the finish; there was reason for him to be thinking it over, because only his quickness of mind had saved him. Those timely taunts, I mean, with which he had blinded and maddened the big man and turned Graem from a human being into a wild bull. What Larry had said had turned out to be true—mere brute force could not down him.

"Joe," he said to me, muttering.

I went with him and took his arm, and, under that pretense, I managed to steady him so that he could walk without a stagger. When I got him well inside the screen of the brush and the trees, he dropped to his knees and was violently sick at his stomach.

I got water for him and bathed his face and his head, on which two big lumps were rising. I give you my word that I worked over him for a whole hour before he was able to sit up. It was still another hour before he was able to stand, and then he walked on, with the bull terrier before him, always looking back as though to read the master's mind.

At the end of the two hours, Larry did his first talking.

"What a man!" he said.

"Yeah, what a man," I said. "Only, he didn't have the brains, just as you said."

"Don't be a fool," said Larry, and he repeated: "What a man!"

"He's a man, all right, and so are you," I said. "You fought like a demon."

"Shut up, Joe," said Decatur. "I hate to hear you talk like this. He almost broke my neck . . . and with what? An overhead blunderbuss, and a short hook that I thought had so little in it, it didn't need a block. And it almost broke my neck!"

He put his hands up to the side of his throat and stood still, then moved his head gingerly from side to side.

"Where did you learn to punch like that?" I asked.

He turned and glared at me. There was no smiling left in him now, for once in his life. "I spent two years in the ring," he snapped. "I thought it would be an easy way of making money, but I got tired of the training. I thought I could go on and lick 'em all, if I worked . . . but that brute, if he knew enough to hold up his hands, could break me into bits in half a minute."

He still massaged his sore neck. I was beginning to appreciate the terrific impact of the blows that Graem had managed to send home, only two punches in the whole brief encounter.

"I had to talk him into an opening," said Larry Decatur. "I tell you what, Joe, I've had some starch and pride taken out of me today. If I go back there, I'll have to face that man-eater, and I'd rather face Satan himself."

"You won't have to face him again," I said.

"I can't face him," said Larry. "If I do, he'll kill me, the next time. One punch of his, if it landed squarely, would smash in a man's ribs and drive the edges of 'em through his heart. What a beast. Tell me about him, Joe."

"He's the straightest shooter, the best fellow, the truest friend, the most generous giver in Alaska," I said. "He's the greatest dog musher and the luckiest miner in the world, too. But he's got one flaw. He's got a bad temper. Sometimes he acts as though he were cracked, just the way he did today."

About this, Larry Decatur thought for some time, then he said: "It was the girl. He's crazy about her. And I don't blame him. If it weren't for the girl, I'd know that I'd never have any trouble with him again."

"The girl won't talk to him," I said. "You don't know her. She saw the fight, but she won't talk to him about it. She's not that kind. She's a peacemaker. She's the finest cut in the world."

"Hush, Joe," he said. "Any fool with half a brain could see that."

"Well," I said, "then how'll she make trouble between the pair of you?"

"I'll wager," said Larry, "that nobody in Alaska has a word to say against her."

"If anybody had a word ever to say against Nelly Bridgeman," I said, "he ain't alive now to repeat it. He died right after he said it, and what he said was buried with him."

Larry Decatur nodded.

"She's that way. A fellow could see that. There's a light that shines out of a good woman . . . if her face is pretty enough to let the light through." He laughed a little at this smart remark of his. "I'm the owner of a boat, now, Joe," he said. "Let's go and have a look at it."

"Before you do that," I said, "suppose that you tell me how you think that the girl could make any trouble between you and Graem?"

"Well, he's crazy about her, isn't he?" he said.

"Yes. Everybody knows that."

"And doesn't everybody know that he wants to marry her?"

"Yes, I suppose that everybody knows that, too, because it's true."

"Well, then, look at it this way . . . today she saw him turned into a ravening brute," said Larry. "And you tell me if any girl with a half-mad father will ever want to marry a man with an insane temper like Graem's?"

"There may be something in what you say," I said, "but I'd hate to think so, Larry, because she's one of the finest girls in the world, and he's one of the finest men. Once she married him, she'd soon know how to manage him. He worships her. She could handle him with a silk thread, in no time at all."

"Is that the fact?" he asked me, with a growl.

"What of it?" I said.

"Well," he muttered, "I'll tell you what . . . before he has her, he'll have to fight me again."

"Hold on, Larry," I said. "You mean to say that you . . . you mean to say that she . . .?"

"I'm going to have her," he said, scowling down at the ground. "I'm going to go straight . . . I want her . . . and I'm going to have her." He looked fiercely up at me. "She likes you, Joe. Will you help me?"

I couldn't help breaking out at him, when I heard Laughing Larry make such a remark.

"I'll see you in torment first," I said.

His right hand twitched into a fist. His scowl blackened.

"Why?" he said.

"You've been a tramp all your life," I said. "You've been a lucky tramp, but you've just been a tramp."

I thought he'd hit me, and I didn't want to be hit by Larry Decatur, after I'd seen him handle Graem. The bull terrier snarled at my feet, looking ready to jump for my throat.

"Steady, Doc," said the master.

He continued to glare at me.

"All right," he said. "You'd be a big help, but I'll make it alone, for that matter. I'll make it all alone." He nodded to himself, as he said this. Then he cleared his brow with a visible effort. He said: "Come on out and we'll look at that boat you were speaking of."

"What will you do with a boat?" I asked him.

"What would I do with Big Ed Graem?" he snapped back. "I'll manage when the time comes, and I've looked it over. I'm walking in luck, this trick. That's what I'm walking in. Don't talk back to me and keep doubting. A little faith is all I need."

I walked on slowly through the woods with him. He was not quite himself. The shock of the blows he had received seemed to have strung him by a finely drawn wire. I sympathized with him, and yet, at the same time, I was afraid of that cunning brain of his almost more than I ever had been afraid of the prodigious strength and the brutal temper of Ed Graem.

He wanted the girl. Perhaps he could get her, too, and who was I, and what power had I to prevent him from having her? It was a gloomy walk for me. I remember, however, that it was on this occasion that I said to him: "Look here, old-timer, how did you keep the terrier from jumping at big Graem in the middle of the fight."

"Why," he said, "didn't you see me wave him off, three or four times?"

"No," I said, "and yet I was watching every move you made, all through the fight."

He seemed surprised, and then he shook his head.

"After all," he said, "the hand is faster than the eye. I've noticed that a good many times in my life before this."

He laughed a little, when he had finished this trite remark, but I didn't like either the remark or the laughter. He seemed to be a fox, and I couldn't help hoping that fox would not get its teeth into poor Nelly Bridgeman, not that I imagined she would be an easy prey of the first clever-tongued man who came her way. No, I had a lot of respect for Nelly and her powers of mind and judgment. Nevertheless, I began to look at the future rather gloomily.

VII

How am I going to give you an idea about this fellow, Larry Decatur? Well, I'll tell you this. When we came out of the woods and crossed the dock, there were half a dozen people in sight, all hunched up, with their hands in their pockets, and they looked at us with a good deal of interest.

"You've made yourself known pretty fast around here, partner," I said to Larry.

He sighed and shook his head.

"That's a bad thing, too," he said. "There's always an advantage in having a card or two up your sleeve. I hate it because I've had to show so much on the first day. Suppose that something takes an important turn, why, I won't have very much ammunition in reserve."

"You mean," I said, "that playing the lazy, worthless bum, you're able to take in a good many people?"

"Brother," he said, "I am."

And he smiled at me in a cheerful and a gentle manner. I noted the smile, but I only nodded at it.

"You know, Larry," I said, "there's such a thing as bein' a ringer."

He cocked his head and smiled at me again. "That's a cheap way of making money," he told me. "I know what you mean, too. But I've never won any big stakes. You can't call me a stake horse."

"A lotta stake horses are never used except for the little money," I said. "The returns are small, but they're sure."

"You're hard on me, Joe," he said.

We stepped into the canoe. There was only one paddle, and there was the weight of the two of us and the dog to handle, besides his pack, which had not yet been taken out of the little craft. But I give you my word that seemed to make no great difference to him. Neither did the wind that was blowing in our teeth. He headed straight out against it to go around to the other side of the dock, and the big, towering stacks of the *Thomas Drayton*. I could feel the fluid, regular, pulsing strokes of the paddle as he drove us along. The man was a machine—a mighty, powerful machine.

Now I get down to what I wanted to tell you in particular.

"Where'd you learn to use a paddle and handle a canoe like this, Larry?" I asked.

I was sitting facing him, watching the dip of his shoulder as he put his weight behind the paddle. The bull terrier, just in front of him, was sitting with its nose in the air and its eyes closed, smelling at the wind.

Larry gave me his smile, which I admired so much and distrusted so much, too.

"Did you ever have the Northwest Mounted Police after you, brother?" he asked.

"What's that got to do with paddling?" I asked. "No, I never had the Northwest Mounted after me."

"If you ever did, you'd know what it has to do with paddling," he said. "Did you ever have the Texas Rangers after you?"

"Yes," I admitted with a shudder. "I had 'em once, and I never wanna have 'em again. I hit the Río Grande and just stepped across it. That's how fast I was traveling south with the Rangers behind me. When they mean business, they sure put a wind in the sail."

"What had you done?" he asked.

"Murder," I answered, "according to what they were told. I had to sit and wait for a while away down in Mexico, until the real crook was caught, and the way was clear for me to come back. I didn't want to see Texas again, so long as the Texas Rangers were after my scalp."

"Well," he said, "I know that the Rangers were a bad lot to mix with, but, at their best, the Rangers were never such a hand-picked lot as the Northwest Mounted. There's something about those people," Larry said, running on, "that puts a chill into your blood. The Rangers are like cowpunchers without a uniform. The Northwest Mounted are like cowpunchers in uniform. It's just as though with the uniform they put on a single character and single qualities. They're all alike. They never get tired riding a horse, walking, or paddling a canoe. They're as much at home in the forest as Indians. They're as much at home in the snow as Eskimos. They all shoot straight and fast. They don't know what it is to be afraid. They all have fast-thinking brains in their heads. And they're all willing to die in the line of duty."

"True," I said. "And the less I have to do with 'em in the line of duty, the better pleased I am."

"You're so right about that, Joe," he said, "that all I can say to you is . . . yes. Now, I happened to run foul of 'em in their line of duty, because I met up with a red-headed scut of a no-good gunman who wore two guns and liked to prove that he was ambidextrous."

"So you ambidextered him into a grave, eh?" I said.

"It was self-defense," said the big fellow, with a little yawn, and another one of his smiles for me, which I was liking less and less. "He was mean in the camp. That's what he was. I'm a fellow, as you know, who always takes a lot, but I was tired from the trail, and I was hunting for peace. I put up with all I could stomach, and finally I told him a few things about the places he could go and the places that he'd probably come from. He was so angry that he made a great mistake. He tried to pull both guns at once, because I'd just been telling him that he was a fake and that all men that pretend they can shoot with both hands were fakes. So he wanted to prove how good he was, and out came both his guns at once."

I remembered how, by talk plus hard punches, this same man had just beaten the great Ed Graem. I said nothing, but did some thinking.

"As a matter of fact, that fellow was ambidextrous," went on Larry Decatur, "and he was fast and straight with both his guns, too. A lot faster than I, but not quite so straight. His right-hand gun knocked the hat off my head, and his left-hand gun shaved off the right side of a pair of mustaches that I was wearing. Though I was a lot slower, and might have been killed by either of those first two shots, except that he was a little hasty and nervous with anger, when I did fire, I split his wishbone right in two. He keeled over and started coughing red, and a little later he was dead."

"And you?" I asked.

"There were a lot of men in that camp that could have said that I fired last, and that I fired in self-defense," said Larry, "but from the foreman to the cook, they were all Canucks, and my observation is that Canucks are an ornery lot."

"You said something," I broke in.

"Thanks," said Larry, with that smile of his again. "Well, then, the Canucks, when the Northwest Mounted came inquiring, showed them the dead man and said who'd killed him. But they said nothing else. And those boys in uniform came for me. I had made a short start on them, but they soon were hot after me. I worked day and night like a beaver. But they had a big advantage. They could all read forest trails and do forest work like Trojans. In addition, they were all white-water men, and I was a green hand with a paddle. For ten days, I had guns and death right behind me all the while. Then I ran into an Indian who was a trapper and who saw by the way that I was cutting across country that I was trying to get away from somebody, so he took up my trail. The long and the short of it was that I had to shoot him, too."

"That makes two dead men so far, Larry," I commented. "Two in one little story."

"The Indian wasn't killed," he said, "just winged in the left arm. When I saw that, and that he couldn't handle his long, old-fashioned rifle, I had an idea. I got hold of that Indian and I gave him first aid, tied up the wound, and treated him kindly.

"Indians are a queer lot. I know that they're cursed out by a lot of the old-timers, but I've always noticed in my treatment of 'em, that if you do a favor for a red man, he always tries to pay you back double, at the least.

"That was what happened this time. He had tried to hunt me down like a moose or a bear. And I'd winged him, and then given him good for evil. He couldn't tell that I'd done it with malice aforethought. He simply felt that I was a great, big, good man. And he bowed down in front of me, so to speak. He showed me the way to his canoe, and, since he couldn't paddle, I had to. I did some funny tricks with that paddle, and nearly upset the canoe in rough water, two or three times, but he sat there and taught me, partly by gestures, partly by words. Mostly by a way he had about him as he crouched in the bottom of the canoe and looked things over. I paddled him five miles, and I learned a whole world of things in that distance about how to handle a canoe and a paddle.

"After that, I lived with the Indian for a month. No, it was two months, but that time passed so happily that it seemed like nothing at all."

"The Northwest Mounted didn't find you, then?"

"They found the cabin, all right," he said, "but I slid up into the attic of the cabin, and the Indian, he stayed down below and lied the way only great artists and Indians can lie. They went away without me, and, though they beat all around that district for about six weeks, they never found me. During that time, I was working the trapline for my friend the Indian, and paddling with him in the canoe, every day, and learning the names of the trees, the birds, and the animals . . . but always paddling. The canoe was our horse and saddle, and we were constantly in it. Well, learning to paddle a canoe is like learning to milk a cow. You may get rusty in the practice, but you'll never quite lose the hang of it, you know."

I nodded my head. "And what came of you and the Northwest Mounted Police, in the end?" I asked.

"Why," he said, "one of the Canucks got to talking over his liquor one day and told the truth about what had happened, and it got to the ears of the Northwest Mounted Police, as everything comes to their ears, sooner or later. So they wiped me off their blacklist, and that's why I'm safe and sound here today. But here we are alongside the *Thomas Drayton*. Do we go up this ladder?"

VIII

We tied up the canoe, and he threw the bull terrier on the deck; after the blood had been washed from his back, you never would have known that he had been in a fight with a Husky, bigger and stronger than any wolf. Then we climbed up to the deck.

It was a pleasant and a sad thing to walk the familiar deck of the old boat. It was pleasant because I could remember so many good runs that we'd had aboard of her. And it was melancholy because every step we made on the deck, the hollow, empty sound from the hull reminded me that she was used up and done for. There was nothing left except to lie here in the lake and rot.

I said so to Larry, and he nodded, smiled at me again, and slapped me on the shoulder.

"I know she's a rotten hulk," he said. "As far as most of the chances go, she's no good at all, I'm sure. But, just the same, a man never knows his luck until it comes up and shouts at his ear. And this thing is so big and cost so little, that I couldn't help picking it up. Let's give it a good look, anyway, and see what it says for itself."

We looked it over from top to bottom. It was as strong and as tight as a clipper ship. There never was a better made river boat in Alaska up to that time. And Larry was delighted.

"She's so fine and big and roomy," he said, "that a fellow could live the rest of his life aboard her, very comfortably . . . and what's so good as a house when you can catch your fish from the roof of it? A thousand dollars for a house like this? It's worth ten thousand for that purpose alone. Joe, I've made an excellent investment."

I only grinned at him and felt sourer than ever.

Then we went into the engine room. When he saw the big engines, he asked more questions than any child. I could explain a lot of things to him, but, of course, I didn't know the scientific details very well. He listened to me more happily than if I had been telling fairy tales.

"You like the *Thomas Drayton*, Joe, don't you?" he said at the last.

"I do," I replied.

"And so do I," he said.

We looked over the accommodations for the passengers and the pilot house, and he fingered the wheel.

"I suppose the touch of a wheel like that would mean a great deal to poor old White-Water Sam, wouldn't it?" he said.

"Him?" I said. "Why, it would start him talking about the *Denver Belle* and throw him into another fit. I guess that's about all."

"I wonder," he said, dreaming the thing over in his mind.

"Maybe you'd like to invite him out here to inspect the ship, eh?" I said, very dry.

"Well, I remember a fellow who was bitten by a rattlesnake and nearly died of it," he said, "and he was half crazy because the country he lived in was full of snakes. He couldn't think of anything else. Life was torment for him for ten years, and he made it torment for his whole family around him. He tried to sell out for a song, but times were so bad that he couldn't sell. His hair turned gray. His years were a misery to him. He got so that he never talked.

"Then, by thunder, another rattler bit him. The instant that the fangs were in him, he forgot all about being afraid of that snake. He reached down and grabbed it by the neck. It bit him a couple more times, but he just bashed its head out on a rock. He didn't die of the poison, either. He was hardly even sick. Perhaps the first dose of poisoning had made him immune. Or perhaps it was a sick snake with withered-up poison glands. I think they come that way, now and then. At any rate, he got over his scare about snakes that way. The next day, he was laughing and joking and telling stories. And the stories that he most liked to tell were all about snakes!"

"And how do you hook up this snake man with old White-Water Sam?" I asked.

"I don't hook him up," said Larry. "I only wanted to show you that you can't tell what will cure and what will kill. But I like this boat, old son, I like it a lot, and I'm glad that I spent a thousand bucks on it. But they must make money with these boats now and then. It cost a penny or two to build this one, and Drayton isn't the man to build a thing just for the fun of it, either."

"Oh, she's made him a hundred thousand net, easy," I said. "And there's some of these things that turn into money faster than that even."

"Are there?" he said, opening his eyes at me.

I remembered, then, and told him the story about a fellow I knew who got wind of a big strike up a river that could be reached from the Yukon by water all the way. When he heard this yarn, he was in Dawson. He knew that he had about an hour before the news would get around all over the place, and he went to the owner of a dirty old scow of a single stacker and bought the boat from him. That tin can of a boat was never worth $5,000, but he had to pay $15,000, and he was glad to do it. Well, she was booked to hold a hundred people, but when the news of the gold strike hit Dawson, everybody wanted to go, and he packed 'em in like sardines. He got two hundred aboard of her for that passage, and he charged 'em $100 a throw. He cleared the whole price of the boat, and more, that first trip. And he came back and did the same thing over and over again, at the same price. Then he sold the hulk for $30,000 and she piled up on a rock the next trip.

When I told Larry these things, it was pretty amusing to see how hard it hit him. There was something childish about him, for all of his foxy cunning, you see.

"Why, in a case like that, with a boat like this, I could pack in four hundred, I suppose," he said. "There must be space for 'em if they're packed in like sardines."

I couldn't help saying: "Well, in a case like that, you'd not be able to pack in any at all, because nobody would have any use for the boat. There's a strike on right now," I said, "and a lot of the boys are running like the mischief to get there. This old boat would be worth her weight in gold, if you could get her through Miles Cañon and what lies below. But you can't get her through, and that's that. She's just . . . well, she's just a houseboat here on Lake Bennett, and I hope you'll enjoy the fishing."

He was not angry. He just shrugged his shoulders.

Finally he said: "You know the only way to do anything in the world, Joe?"

"Work like the mischief and never spend a cent. Is that what you mean?" I asked.

He shrugged his shoulders again. "You won't listen to me," he said, "but I could tell you something that's worth knowing about."

"Go on and tell me, partner," I said, "because I'm anxious to know."

"You're not anxious," he said, "but I'll tell you anyway. I'll give this away free. The only way to get along is to read fairy stories, and then try like a demon to make 'em come true."

"And how do you try to make 'em come true?" I asked, grinning at him.

"By believing in 'em when you hear 'em," he replied.

I laughed a good deal at that.

He walked around the *Thomas Drayton* for a while longer. Everything he saw, he admired—the strength of the planking along the decks, for instance, the size of the anchors, and the thickness of the tarred ropes that were coiled under tarpaulins. I must say for Tom Drayton that his ship was trim, fore and aft, and ready to go. I liked Larry better and better, just because he admired the old craft so much.

After a while, he said that he was going to sleep on board her that night, and he said to me: "What are you doing now?"

"Eating and sleeping," I said.

"Want a job?"

"Sure," I said.

"Water job?"

"That suits me to the ground."

"Then I'll hire you. You're captain, crew, and skipper, pilot, and engineer, and all the other names. You're the crew of the *Thomas Drayton*."

I laughed.

"I mean it," he said. "You get a hundred dollars a month till I find something else to do with the boat. When I find a way of using her, I'll pay you more."

"When you find a way of using her?" I questioned. "You'll never find a way, brother. Don't you go and waste a hundred dollars a month on me for nothing. You don't even need a night watchman out here. Nobody's going to try to steal your boat . . . nobody but you wants her."

"You let me run it my own way," he said. "Only, Joe, you promise that you'll stick with the boat, no matter what happens, for a month, eh?"

"Of course," I said. "But what can happen? If a storm blows up, I might run another line ashore. But there'd be nothing else to do."

"Well, whatever I want to do with her, you'll stick with her for the month?" he asked again.

I laughed again. "I'll do that," I said. "I don't mind a vacation on a hundred a month of anybody's money. I'll even shine brass for that, but there's no brass 'board the *Thomas Drayton*."

We hoisted his kit aboard the boat, and stowed it in the captain's cabin, which was big and fine, a real bedroom, with a real double bed in it, such as a man could twist around in, and still have leg and head room.

Larry liked that cabin fine, too.

Then we crossed the deck, and, with the dog behind us, we ran a plank out to the dock and stepped ashore.

Old Steve Mannock was sitting on a pile of rain-stained wood, chewing tobacco, with his arms folded on his chest, his beard working up and down as he chewed.

He was looking at us rather glassy-eyed, the way a man does when he's chewing at tobacco and thinking of nothing at all.

I said: "Here's the new owner of the *Thomas Drayton*, Steve. This is Lawrence Decatur. Larry, this is Steve Mannock, the best engineer that ever tied down a safety valve and blew steam in the face of a gale."

Steve got up and shook hands with Larry. He didn't seem much impressed about his owning the boat, but he looked him up and down and said: "So they tell me that you licked Big Ed Graem in a fair fight."

"I say nothing about fighting. I don't like fights," said Larry Decatur.

"You don't, eh?" said Steve Mannock, fingering his beard and looking very thoughtful.

"No, I don't," said Larry.

"Well," said Steve, "nobody ever brought a bull terrier this far north without liking to see a fight. That dog'll freeze when the winter comes on."

"Run your thumb down his back against the grain," said Larry.

Steve did it, although Larry had to hold the dog's head while he was being thumbed.

Well, that coat was as thick and soft as a seal's fur. You couldn't even see the pink of the skin.

"I'm blowed," said Steve. "Is this a bull terrier cross on a white seal?"

"What are you doing now, Steve?" said Larry.

"I'm aiming at a long mush and a dry mush," said Steve. "And I hate dry land!"

"You stay here and be the engineer of the *Thomas Drayton* for a month, at a hundred dollars for the term," Larry proposed.

"And what will the *Thomas Drayton* be doing all that month?" asked Steve.

"Thinking it over and resting your feet," suggested Larry. "But if you want the job, you've got to shake hands to stay with her, no matter what I do with her."

Steve looked up and down the lake. Then he laughed. "Yeah," he said, "I don't mind resting my feet for a month. I don't mind, either, shaking the hand that knocked Big Ed cock-eyed. He had it coming to him."

IX

Jeff Worth came down the dock, just then, with a light in his eye. I knew by that that somebody else was burning up; Jeff never had a light of his own.

He came up to Larry and said: "Decatur, I've got some news for you."

"Good or bad?" Larry said.

"Why, good news, I guess it is," replied Jeff. "Big Ed is over in the Bridgeman saloon with five thousand dollars in dust to pay you."

"Waiting for me . . . to pay it . . . is he?" said Larry.

"Yes, that's it," said Jeff. "Coming over now?"

"All right. You can tell him that I'm coming," said Larry.

"I was gonna tell you the same thing," said Steve Mannock. "But Jeff always gets his fingers in the other fellow's pie."

"He means trouble," I told Larry. "If Big Ed is back in that saloon, he's got poison in him."

"I could tell that if he were on the other side of the earth," said Larry. "I didn't think that he was in there to tell me how much he loved me."

Straight off, he starts walking down the dock toward the saloon. Steve and I followed.

"Did he lick Big Ed fair and square?" Steve asked in a murmuring voice.

I thought back to the fight. Well, it had been a fair fight, all right. It was a fair fight when Young Corbett fought terrible Terry McGovern and drove him insane with banter, so that he fought blindly and was knocked out. It was a fair fight. And using the same weapons, Larry might meet and beat the great Graem again, that mountain of a man. Still, it was hardly a fair test, according to what I knew of the way a real fight ought to be carried out.

"It was a pretty fair fight. He talked Big Ed out of a couple of points, maybe," I said. "But it was a pretty fair fight."

"If a man can use his tongue along with his fists," said Steve, "it's just a sign that he has brains, and brains are more important than hands in winning any kind of a fight, I reckon."

There was something in that. It was about what Larry had said before the battle ever had a start.

We walked into the saloon behind Larry, and there at the far end of the counter was Big Ed, looking like thunder—purple thunder, at that. I never saw such a jaw on any man. It was puffed out on both sides of the chin, where those raps of Larry had cracked home. There was no other mark on his face. Larry was such a marksman that, when he played for the face, he had hit nothing but the button.

Graem said: "I've come to pay you your bet." He pointed to a canvas sausage that lay on the bar. There would be about fifteen to seventeen pounds of gold in that sausage to pay a $5,000 debt. You remember that he had made the bet at ten to one.

I looked at the back of Larry's head, and wondered what he would say and do. I was glad that Nelly Bridgeman was out of the room and that her father, apparently recovered from his attack of hysterics, was there in place to serve drinks. He looked with his mild, rather dim eyes from face to face, not understanding anything.

But the rest of the room was pretty well filled. Everybody within reach was there to see what happened the second time Big Ed met up with the cheechako.

I think there was a good deal of sympathy for Graem, now. After he had been licked, people felt better about him. They were more willing to remember the bigness of his heart and the good things that he had done from the White Horse to Nome.

I had some of those feelings, I know, as I looked at his bruised and swollen jaw.

"There's five thousand dollars in dust in that poke," said Graem. "Come and take it."

There was a challenge in his way of saying this, as though he dared the other fellow to take it at his own risk.

I saw the risk well enough. Anybody who reached for the money would be within the grip of one of those huge hands, and, although Larry might be able to beat Graem in a fair fist fight, he would be crumpled like a bunch of dead leaves in the grip of that giant.

I suppose Larry saw it, too. I saw him halt, one elbow leaning against the bar. Nobody else was there at the bar. The rest were backed up around the room, looking on. They were the audience, and they were expecting some action. They got what they were not looking for.

"That money is not mine because I never make a bet on myself except at evens," Larry said. "That money is not yours because you were fool enough to take on the fight at those odds. Give it to Bridgeman, to dole out to the boys when they come by and need a grubstake or a free drink or a hand-out of some kind."

You see, it kept him out of the reach of the hand of Graem. Also, it made Graem give over the money to another man, a man from whom he couldn't afford to keep it. In the third place, it put Larry more in the right than ever, and it put Graem more in the wrong, in some way, as if he should have had impulses as generous as that without being forced to it. Finally it wound up the whole argument, and there was nothing to do, you would have said, except for Ed to pay over the money, and then walk out of the saloon.

It was a facer and it was a silencer.

Larry turned around toward the bar and he took out some money. Over his shoulder he called to the crowd: "Come on, boys, and liquor on me! I haven't had a real drink today!"

I suppose that everybody in the place wanted to hold back still in order to see what might happen between Graem and Larry, but the speech that Larry had made in the first place and his way of throwing Graem out of the picture in the second put everything at an end, as it seemed, and the whole gang came shouldering in toward the bar.

But nobody, I noticed, came very close to big Graem. He stood there like a frozen thundercloud at the end of the bar, emitting rays of darkness and icy cold.

Altogether, it was a great play that Larry had made. It had cost him $5,000, to be sure. It had cost him so much that I had to replan and resketch all of my ideas of him on the spot, and the job sprained my brain.

It was also a complete flabbergasting for Graem.

I heard Steve Mannock murmuring at my ear: "That fellow is something worth having in Alaska. He'll find something worthwhile, or else he'll wreck the territory hunting for it."

I was inclined to think that this might be the truth.

Then I heard old Bridgeman speaking. He was a gentleman, even if his grammar was not perfect. Neither is mine, for that matter, and neither is yours, perhaps, if you dig down to the bottom. I never could see what difference the words made, so long as the meaning was clear.

White-Water Sam said: "Boys, this is a pretty big thing for a cheechako to do. This drink ain't on him. A man like him can't buy the first drink in my place, because just now I'm thinking of a lot of the boys that come through here, dead beat and all down and out. They've had bad luck coming in or they've had bad luck going out. They get here with their hearts sick. It's a bad thing when the sickness gets as deep down as the heart, I wanna tell you. I been sick at the heart myself. I once heard a story about a boat called the *Denver Belle*."

"Say, Sam," I yelled out, "get back to the point! If Decatur doesn't pay for the drink, who does?"

I was sweating when I said it, but it had the right effect. It switched him from the bad point and got him across the bridge to a new idea.

He looked down the bar and smiled at me. "Hello, Uncle Joe," he said. He called me that from hearing Nelly so often. "I didn't see you before, son. I'll tell you who pays for the drink. I do! It's on the house. Fill 'em up, boys, and all to the brim!"

He spun the bottles down the bar, and everybody filled. Everybody except Ed Graem.

Everybody filled to the brim, too.

"Here's to Larry Decatur!" called old Sam.

And we put up a roar and put down the drink.

Only Graem did not drink. And then I saw him striding straight toward Larry, through the crowd.

X

I gave Larry a nudge in the ribs hard enough to break a couple of them, but he paid no attention until the hand of Big Ed was stretched out and about to fall on his shoulder. Then Decatur wheeled around like a spinning top, and shoved a gun straight into the stomach of Ed Graem.

Guns were unfamiliar things in northern Alaska, you know. That is to say, revolvers were. A rifle might be worth its weight for hunting game, but a revolver was just a dead burden that hardly ever repaid its keeping. Men who were used to counting not only the pounds by the ounces that they loaded onto their dog sleds were not likely to carry any extras.

So it gave a shock to Graem when that gun was pulled on him. You could see the shock hit him between the eyes, as it were, and the hand that he had stretched toward the shoulder of Larry jumped back again as though it had been burned.

"What d'you mean?" demanded the big man, snarling.

"I'll tell you what I mean," said Larry. "I won't have any more trouble with you. I've thrashed you once," he said, with a slow and deliberate contempt, "and I'm not going to break up my hands hammering you on the jaw again. If you try to lay a hand on me once more, I'll shoot your wishbone in two. Understand?"

Graem stood back and dropped his hands into the deep pockets of his coat, his face working spasmodically.

At last he said: "It's guns that you want, is it?"

"It's peace that I want," said Larry Decatur, "and it's peace that I'm going to have. You've been a Juggernaut, and rolled over people long enough. Now you're going to learn to back up and keep in your place, or I'll fit you into a grave before your time comes."

It was pretty mean talk, any way that you looked at it. But by the stern quiet that came over that room, and the hard way the people all looked at Graem, I could see that Larry had uttered their own thoughts for them. They were tired of Graem's overbearing ways, and they were glad to have a spokesman to utter their opinion.

Graem, with a flash across the faces of the crowd, must have seen just where he stood, and what he saw sickened him more even than the beating he had received not so long before on this same day. I suppose that he had always excused himself, admitting to his conscience that he had a bad temper, and all that, but reasonably sure that his good deeds performed in the north country far more than overbalanced the evil of his wild passions.

Now he saw the truth, and it was as though half of his lifetime of work had been thrown away.

He went right out from the saloon without lifting his hand or his voice. He simply walked out of the picture.

Well, when we had seen Graem budge from where he had been standing, I don't think that any of us could believe our eyes and ears.

No one spoke, as Larry put up his gun, but finally Denny Lawson, a red-headed, no-account, lazy loafer that carried a bad name in the States with him, this red-headed Lawson, standing in a corner of the saloon, broke out into bawling laughter, and a traveling mate of his, a blinking, down-headed rat called Lefty, he laughed, too.

"That's the finish of the great Graem," said Lawson. "Curse him. He's had his foot on our necks long enough, I say."

"He's had it a lot too long," said Lefty, the echo.

And they walked out of the room together, laughing together, and that laughing sounded like the snarling of two dogs, which was what they were.

"If they fool about with Ed Graem," said Larry Decatur, as calm as could be, "they'll get themselves broken up, I tell you. He's not broken, as they think. He's only holding himself, and piling up strength inside of himself, like water piling behind a dam that's sure to break."

I felt the same way about it, and I really hoped, if those two hounds bothered him, Big Ed would put his hands on them.

Old White-Water Sam was troubled. He didn't know what it was all about. He'd missed, as usual, a good many links in the chain of happenings, and he began to ask questions now, but we soon soothed him and told him that everything was all right. He was as easy to handle, most of the time, as a well-raised child. And he was soon smiling at us, with his very kind and half-vacant eyes.

He liked to have the boys about him. The saloon business was nothing to him, except a chance to keep company around.

And I've never known him to ask for the price of a drink. Any bum could go in there and drink all day and never pay a cent, except that, when the other boys found out about it, they skinned the tramp alive. No, White-Water generally got his money, but never by collecting it.

Pretty soon, Larry Decatur left the saloon, with me and Steve Mannock going along.

Outside, Larry said: "I want you fellows to know that I'm sorry for the trouble I've had with Graem. I don't want to shame him and I don't want to break him. I hate to pull a gun. But one fight a day with a grizzly bear is about enough for me."

Steve Mannock said that nobody could possibly blame him, that everything he had done was all right, and that he had admired the way that Larry had handled the ticklish job. But I didn't say a word. Because it seemed to me that Larry was a little too deep for me to appreciate him altogether. So I said nothing, and then felt the quizzical eyes of Larry resting on me.

He said, if we wanted to, we could put our blankets aboard the old *Thomas Drayton*; he had something else on hand. So he went one way, and we got our duds and blanket rolls and went out to the boat.

It was good to step back on board of her, and Steve Mannock said: "I'll tell you what's wrong with life on shore. There ain't any run to it. There ain't any get-up and get to it. A dog team is all right, but a dog team has to stop at night. But a river, it don't stop at night. It keeps on going, and it snakes you along the right way, smooth as silk, or else it comes smash ag'in' the bows, all night long. There ain't any finer thing in the world, from my way of thinking, than to hear an engine growl low and growl high, working all oily and shiny, never letting up, never getting tired, grinding up ag'in' a current. That's the life for me."

I couldn't help agreeing with him, except that for me engines were interesting because they were what kept the ship trembling and the paddle wheel crashing around; it was the way of the ship itself that I wanted to follow.

Steve and me, we tidied up a little, and then came out and smoked our pipes on the forward deck. Tom Drayton sauntered out and sat on the lumber pile and talked to us a while.

"What kinda voyages you boys going to sail in that old boat?" he asked.

Steve Mannock, he took and tamped down the coal in the bowl of his pipe, and worked up a good head of smoke. Then he said through the white mist of it: "I'll tell you, Tom. We're aiming to make a great big kite, and we're gonna make that kite with a frame of whole trees, joined together, and we're going to stretch number one sailcloth all over the frame, and make a real kite of it, d'ye see?"

"And then?" says Drayton, grinning and waiting.

"Then we're gonna wait for a stiff wind to blow up, like it does around here, now and then. And that wind will hoist up our kite and make it jump into the sky."

"Go on," said Tom Drayton. "And how you going to anchor that kite to the ground?"

"That's the point, brother," said Steve. "We don't want to anchor it. We just want to get it flying high and strong, with a coupla strong cables hitched onto it, and then we'll fasten those cables onto the old *Thomas Drayton*, and we'll let the kite go, and it'll lift this old ship right out of Lake Bennett and across the rapids. When we get above the open river on the farther side, we'll cut the cables and the kite will go sailing on toward the infernal regions and the North Pole, and the *Thomas Drayton*, it'll drive down easy and graceful, like a wild duck taking to the water, and there we'll be floating in open water, and nothing to do but to make money."

"That's a good idea," says Tom Drayton, "and it's a blasted shame that I didn't have it. Because it's the only way that you'll ever get the old boat into water where she'll be worth her salt."

"Yeah, it's the only way," said Mannock. "But you see that a gent can nearly always get what he wants, if he just puts his mind to it."

"There's few minds like yours, brother," says Drayton.

This was true. There were not very many like old Steve Mannock.

Well, he chatted with us a while longer. Then, because it was getting along toward the right time for supper, he went back inland, and Steve suggested that we start up a fire in the galley and he'd be the fireman, while I went and got some provisions together for the cooking of supper.

It sounded like a good idea to me, because grub eaten on deck always tastes better than grub eaten on shore.

So I went over to the store and got some bacon and coffee and things. When I came out, with the package under my arms, I heard the voice of Nelly Bridgeman, laughing sort of sweet and low, as it says in the song. And there she was, saying good bye to Larry Decatur. He was laughing, too, and I never had heard him laugh like that before.

He went down the dock toward the boat, carrying something, and I met up with the girl as she started back toward her father's saloon. She waved to me and hailed me, and I pulled up for to find out what she wanted.

"Uncle Joe," she said, "he's a wonderful fellow, isn't he?"

"Who's a wonderful fellow?" I said, knowing mighty well what she meant.

"You know," she said. "It's Larry that I mean."

"You mean Decatur, do you?" I said.

"Of course, I mean him. And isn't he wonderful?"

"I know Decatur," I said, "but I don't know anything about him being wonderful."

She stepped up to me and hooked an arm through one of mine, and she said: "Stop scowling like that, Uncle Joe."

"I'm plagued if I'm your uncle," I said, "and I'm plagued if I stop scowling."

"What's the matter, Uncle Joe?" said Nelly.

"Are you going and getting yourself all dizzy about Larry Decatur?" I asked.

"Perhaps I am," she replied. "And why not? What's wrong with that?"

She was so frank and so straight about it, that I felt worse than ever, you can imagine, a girl like her and a clever, worldly fox like Larry Decatur!

"Nothing's wrong with it," I said. "It just goes to show that practice makes perfect, as the saying is."

"What sort of practice?" she said.

"Why, with women," I said. "No matter where he goes, he always leaves three or four girls breaking their hearts after him. He's just that way. He's learned the hang of 'em. He knows how to look at 'em, and how to speak at 'em so's all their nerves go jumping together."

"D'you know what he's been talking to me about?" she asked.

"No," I said, "but I can guess."

"You'd guess wrong," she said. "He's been telling me about an old prospector he knew down in Mexico, and the way that they lived together and all of that."

"I know," I said. "I've heard that yarn, too. There's natural liars, and there's improved natural liars. And he's one of the improved kind."

"Don't you think it's true?" she said.

"The truth don't interest Larry," I said. "Why should it, with the kind of a mind that he's got, ready to improve on nature?"

"You don't like him?" she said.

"Oh, he's all right," I said.

"Right down in your heart, I can see that you're fond of him," she said. "Now, you confess like a good fellow."

"Dog-gone it, Nelly," I said, "I'm scared of him, to tell you the truth. He's a good fellow, but I'm scared of him. His mind works too far ahead of mine."

XI

She wanted to talk to me some more about Larry, but I broke away, and told her that I wouldn't stand there and waste my time on her.

Then, when I was a step away, I turned around, came back to her, and shook a finger at her, as I said: "Look here, young woman, and listen to me."

"I'm listening, Uncle Joe," she said.

She tried to swallow down the laughing and be serious, and she got rid of all the laughing, but not of the happy smile that was the tag end of it.

"Don't you go playing around with Larry Decatur," I warned. "Larry is all right. But he's not all right for you. He wants to amuse himself a little. He hates lonely evenings, and all that. He wants to sit around and talk. No harm in that. Only, you watch out you don't believe what he says."

"All right. I'll watch," she said.

And she began to laugh again, and her eyes shone and brooded on me rather fondly, as if I was an old and foolish fellow, what they call a character in a book.

Well, I broke away from her again, at that, and I went out to the ship, where I found that a mist had gathered off the lake around her, and she looked wetter and more gloomy and more hopeless, except that now, out of one smokestack, there was a little thin twist of smoke rising and boring its way up through the air.

That gave life to her. It made you think of the big fires roaring and fuming under the boilers, with such a force of draft that the whole ship trembled with the whipping of the flames. I knew that no such thing was happening, and I knew that there was no chance for the *Thomas Drayton* to get away from her mooring. Just the same, I was interested, as I stood there in the fog, and looked up at the black pair of shadows that were the stacks, and saw the smoke spiral coming out of one of them.

Just the fire in the galley, of course, but it meant more than that to me. It meant the stir of the ghost of something in me.

When I went aboard, I found Larry and Steve at the galley door, and the fire booming and roaring in the stove inside. Larry was holding a big bucket and he was saying: "Mister Engineer, I hope you won't mind going over the side and painting out the name of this boat, fore and aft?"

"Look here, Decatur," the engineer said, "you know that it ain't luck to sail on a ship that's got no name?"

"Oh, she's going to have a new name, all right," said Larry. "Don't you worry about that, brother. She'll have a new name, and a beauty, too."

"*Humph,*" Steve said, and looked at him very suspicious.

But he went aft to rig a platform and drop it over the side, and, while I undid the chuck and began to fix for cooking it, Decatur, he hung around and sniffed and said that it looked pretty good to him and he'd join us at supper that night.

"She'll cook better than I do," I said. "You better go and eat with her."

"I better go and eat with who?" Decatur asked.

"Why, with Nelly Bridgeman," I responded.

"What are you driving at, brother?" he said.

"I've just been talking to her," I said. "She wanted to stand and gossip about you. Asked me if I didn't think that you're wonderful, is what she asked me."

He chuckled. "I can guess what you said," he replied.

"I didn't say much," I said. "Only that I knew you pretty well and didn't know anything wonderful about you. I told her some other things, but it didn't make any difference. She kept on getting more and more of a calf look in her eyes. Look here, Larry, don't you go and try any of your smooth ways on her. You take some of your lingo and check it in the freight room, will you?"

He only regarded me with a calm and critical eye. Then he said: "You're all right, Joe. You're a fellow to tie to."

He said no more, and I thought that I'd talked my mind freely enough.

Well, we had supper, all three of us, and talked about river work and such things. Then Steve and me went over the side and painted out the name *Thomas Drayton* on the stern, and went forward and hooked the same platform over the bows and painted out the name there, too.

Big Larry Decatur, he walked up and down on the dock in the dim light with the fog rolling in thicker and thicker all the while.

He said, with the new name that he was going to put on that boat with his own hands, she'd become famous, and she'd bring in more money than you could shake a stick at.

"How'll you make money with her?" asked Steve Mannock.

"Where there's a will there's a way," he said.

Afterward, Steve said to me: "You think that he's got any real idea of what he's going to do with the *Thomas Drayton?*"

"She's not the *Thomas Drayton* now," I corrected. "She's nothing but a boat waiting for a name. This morning, I don't think that he had more than a ghost of an idea, when he bought her, I mean, but in the meantime I guess that his brain has been working overtime. He may have an idea, hazy and thin. Look at the way he's walking back and forth. He's got some scheme in his mind. That's the way with him. Then, the painting out of this here name . . . I dunno what that means exactly, but it's not just for fun. It's done for a purpose, though perhaps he himself doesn't exactly know yet where the idea will end. He's fumbling his way along through the dark, but he'll come out into the open before very long, I guess."

We finished our job on deck again, hoisted up the painting platform, and stowed it. Then we washed the paint off our hands with turpentine and tried to get the stink of the turpentine off with soap and water.

Then we made our bunks down aft, in opposite cabins, one for the chief engineer and one for the mate. There was a narrow passage in between.

We opened the portholes, and a wind came down the lake and drove a steady stream of fog through them, filling the whole inside of the ship with mist. It was as white as the foam of milk in the lantern light.

We smoked a pipe apiece, yarning with one another through the open doors of our cabins, but after a time Steve failed to answer back, so I guess that he was asleep.

I put out the lantern and tried to go to sleep in my turn, but, just as I was shutting my eyes, I began to think of the fight between Larry and Big Ed, and that thought brought my eyes wide open again. I lay there and saw the whole fight through once more, from beginning to end, every blow that was struck.

After that, there were other things to think about—the walk and talk with Larry, the buying of the ship, the second meeting with Big Ed Graem, the retelling of White-Water Sam's yarn, and a lot of other things, winding up with the bright, happy, foolish look that I had seen in the eyes of Nelly Bridgeman.

Well, when I got that far, I'd been twisting and turning back and forth so often on my bunk that the blankets were in ridges and knots, so I got up to straighten them. And, as I did this, the wind blew the fog into my lungs and my head, if you know what I mean, and I decided that I'd dress and go on deck for a turn.

I did that, and on deck found the wind singing and howling by turns, though not as loudly as it had done through the hull of the ship below. I took a few turns up and down, and then stood in the face of the gale near the paddle box and watched the fog thinning under the blast of the wind, then coming on again quite thicker than ever and dwindling once more.

I was still there, getting cold and stiff and about to start pacing once more, when I thought I saw, well forward, something gray, moving slower than the blowing of the fog, that came in over the rail from the dock side of the ship.

At that, I shook my head, and just as I was about to shrug the idea out of my mind, I saw another bundle of gray go over the rail from the dock, and made out, pretty accurately, the form of a man walking up the deck, going forward, and disappearing in a thicker gust of the blowing mist.

XII

Danger, I think, has all sorts of faces, but it has only one effect, and that's a cold fist in the stomach and a cold wriggling up the center of the spine.

I had that fist in the stomach and that cold lightning up the spine and into the base of the brain as I saw the second form go forward. For one thing, the figure was moving at a stalking pace. I could make that out. It was bent over, and it went step by step, the way a man does when he's listening in between his own footfalls.

I wished that I had a gun on me. But if I went below for one, it might be too late to look in on whatever mischief was on hand. Steve Mannock was an oldish chap, but I wished that I had him with me, too, if only for company's sake. However, I couldn't wait to get Steve any more than I could wait to get the gun; I had to sneak forward along the deck.

Where had they gone, and what were they doing? What was there to do on board the old *Thomas Drayton* at this hour and in this weather? There was not much on board that was worth the stealing. And there was nobody of any consequence on board, except, perhaps, big Larry Decatur, now probably soundly sleeping in the captain's cabin.

Anyway, it was for the cabin that I went.

I pulled off my boots to make less noise. I pulled off my Mackinaw, too, because stiff cloth ties you up around the shoulders and elbows at a time when you may need all your strength and speed.

And now I sneaked forward and went down the companionway, shuddering not with the cold of the wind, but with the ice that had gathered around my own heart. I felt my forty years, too, and wished that I could throw ten of them, at least, over my shoulder.

I got down and forward along the narrow little passage in time to see a glint of light before me, and that light showed me two forms standing there more than half shrouded in the mist which, as I said before, had blown all through the ship, and seemed even thicker inside than outside. The light showed me that there were two men, and it showed me that they were standing outside the captain's door.

The light went out and somehow I knew that the door had opened, and that the two of 'em had gone in together, or one right after the other.

That was enough for me. I let out a yell that half deafened me, being thrown back, as it was, from the walls of the passage on either side, and I started to run forward.

Another yell, like the roar of a lion, answered me, half stifled, then I heard a sharp, high-pitched screech. Just as I thought I had reached the captain's door, a body smashed into me and knocked me flat. I grabbed a pair of legs that kicked and wriggled. I worked up higher and found myself grappling with the body and arms of a very sinewy, desperately twisting man, who cursed steadily, half under his breath.

He was not quite a match for me, though. I got a good grip, and, remembering some of the wrestling tricks of my school days, I slipped a half-nelson on him that made the bones of his neck fairly creak.

A light glimmered behind me. Then, I heard the voice of Larry—never anything so welcome!—saying: "It's all right. Let him get up."

So I stood up. I looked back, and saw Larry holding, by the nape of the neck, that rat of a Lefty, and there on the deck lay red-headed Denny Lawson.

The free hand of Larry held the hoop of a lantern, and a big Colt revolver.

When Denny Lawson got up, he stood twisting and turning, first toward Larry and then toward another gun that lay at a little distance from him. It must have jolted out of his hand when he bumped into me and went down.

"Stick up those hands, brother," said Larry Decatur. "Joe, get that gun and poke the muzzle of it into redhead's ribs, will you?"

I did what I was told to do, then we marched the pair up to the pilot house, where old Steve Mannock came running to meet us with a ship's axe in his hand. He had heard the uproar, and had thought that he was waking up into a bad nightmare.

However, he had grabbed the axe and tracked down the disturbance by the shining of Larry's lantern.

When Steve saw the two rats and heard how they'd been caught, I almost thought that he would brain the two of them with the axe.

You know, Steve was an old-timer, and the old-timers in Alaska were not ones to put up with crime. There was enough trouble with weather and starvation and all that, without having murder floating around in the air. They simply wouldn't be bothered by such nuisances.

I managed to herd Steve away from the pair, but he had swung that axe high enough to throw a terrible chill into both of them. Lefty simply dropped to his knees and cowered in a corner.

Then Larry said: "Now, you two, what were you after? You had nothing against me, so far as I know. Somebody in the south send you on my trail for a price?"

Lefty could not talk, his teeth were chattering so hard and so fast.

Denny Lawson was hardly in better shape, but he managed to stammer out that they hadn't come north to get Larry.

"Then what brought you on board tonight. You meant to bump me off, didn't you?" said Larry.

Lawson started to say no, and then stopped himself. Of course, it was as clear as anything in the world that he had come on board for that very purpose. It couldn't have been robbery that he had in mind, and for what else except robbery or murder would two fellows come with guns, as he and Lefty had done?

Larry helped him out a little.

He said: "I could take you fellows down the docks and get the boys together, and let them know how we found you here. How long would you last then?"

There was not much doubt about what would have happened to them. They looked at one another, those two rascals, and said nothing, but looked a great deal.

Then Larry said: "On the other hand, you can tell me what made you come after me. And it might be interesting enough to make me turn you loose. You feel more like talking now?"

Lefty burst out, all of a shudder and a shake: "It was Big Ed!"

That was a shock to me. Ed Graem had sent hired men to do a murder for him? It didn't fit into the picture that all Alaska had in its mind's eye of that man.

Yet, Larry surprised me by saying, bluntly: "If you want me to believe that Ed hired you boys for the job, I'll tell you that you're lying."

Said Denny Lawson: "You know, chief, that it wasn't because he'd promised us any money, but all that he can think about is you, and all that he can do is to wander around and walk up and down, and, whenever your name is mentioned, he pretty near busts loose. I never seen anybody half so hot about anything as he is about you. So it seemed to me and to Lefty, here, that if we turned a trick that pleased him a lot, he'd be pretty good to us. Money's nothing to Big Ed. He'd make the way easy. We come on board sort of intending to look things over and . . . ."

He cringed as he said it. It was about the worst confession that I'd ever heard from anybody's lips. But from my point of view, nearly all gunmen are bad actors to begin with, and cowards before they're through. They're bad actors, because they know that they can handle a gun a lot better than the other man, and they're cowards because if they bump into a tight fit where their gun work won't help them out, they've no idea what to do with themselves. They're like strangers in foreign countries, not able to speak a word.

Steve Mannock growled and cursed. He said that he'd never heard of worms being able to crawl that far north without being killed by the weather, and that it was time for this pair to be exposed.

I know that Steve would have killed them offhand, without a thought, but Larry had given his word to that precious pair, and he kept it.

He simply said: "You boys can go, but there's only one direction for you to travel in. That's south. Get out of the country. Go back to wherever you belong, for you don't belong up here. I'm going to inquire, from time to time, and, if I hear your names north of the White Horse, I'm going to look you up and I'll look you up with a fine-toothed comb. Understand? Now get on shore!"

They went, all right. On the verge of the plank to the dock, that fellow Lefty, the sneak, had the nerve to turn around and beg for his gun, because he said that without a gun he was like a man with his head cut off.

Steve Mannock, for an answer, picked up a chunk of wood and slung it at him and hit him on the seat of the pants. He pretty nearly fell off the plank, and made the edge of the dock in one jump and one long howl. I wasn't amused. Neither was

Steve. But as we stood there, watching the pair soak out of sight in the mist, big Larry Decatur said: "Boys, I appreciate what you've done and the way that you've stood by me. It makes me want to tell you what I've got in my mind, and everything that I've planned. But there are a lot of reasons, nearly all selfish, why I can't say a word to a living soul. Understand?"

I said that I understood, and Steve Mannock grunted that a man that was worth anything kept his own business to himself. He wanted to know what the plan was for the boat, but he wouldn't talk about it; he wouldn't ask any more questions.

Then we got the next jolt.

For Larry said: "You fellows go and finish out your sleep. Then, when you're ready, go ashore and hunt up some boys who are looking for a couple of days' work. Pay them anything you like. You can buy good, dry wood as cheap as dirt. Buy plenty of that, too, and load it into the bunkers. And, Mannock, you get up steam as fast as you can, and look over the engine with your grease can and oil pot, will you?"

XIII

It isn't often that one can speak of a chill of interest going through a person, far less a whole community, but that's what happened in that whole gang of interested people. When Mannock and I went on shore to drum up a crew, we had the whole bunch to pick from. It was true that everybody was more than half scared, but it was also true that everybody was nearly crazy with excitement.

That silly yarn of Mannock's, about making the great kite and hitching the whole body of the *Thomas Drayton* to it, was actually seriously repeated, believe it or not!

I heard four men speaking of it in the saloon, and they were more than half in earnest, and they wanted to know what I thought of the scheme and was anybody crazy enough to attempt it? Then they got to talking about the lifting power of a strong wind, and before long they were defending the scheme not as a probable one, but as a possibility.

Well, as I was saying, we got our crew together and started them to work, loading wood onto the ship and packing some supplies on board. We didn't need much food, said Larry Decatur. Once the real work started, he added, eating and drinking was not what people would be interested in.

He said this with a smile that I've never forgotten to this day.

We were busy getting the ship ready. The fires were built up and the smoke went shooting up through the stacks. Now and then, Mannock turned the engines over and tuned 'em up, oiling and greasing to his heart's content, till he was as shiny and black as a greased pig, from head to foot.

We did this work in the same fog of which I've spoken. I've never seen before or since such a fog in Alaska. Of course, it wasn't a sea mist, at that distance from the sea. It was simply a long exhalation from the water and the marsh land, brought on I don't know by what, perhaps some change of temperature. There had been dense fog even when the wind was blowing. Now the wind had fallen and, of course, the mist was thicker than ever. It got so that you could hardly recognize a man at eight or ten feet.

While we were fixing things aboard the ship, our boss had the painting platform slung over the bows, and he went to work with the paintbrush and painted in a new name. Then he went aft and painted the name again on the paddle box.

Nobody paid much attention to what he was doing. I think nearly everybody took it for granted that he was simply repainting the old name more clearly, the *Thomas Drayton*. And because they thought that, they didn't look at his work.

But I looked at it, and what do you think that I saw, after I'd walked back and forth for a long time, and peered through the mist?

He had painted, in place of the old name, *Denver Belle!*

Why, it packed ice all around my heart, and I had the first dim, far-off inkling of what might be in the mind of Larry Decatur. However, I put the thing far away from me. It was too crazy, too impossible.

When Larry had finished his job, I got hold of him and said: "None of the boys have noticed what you painted on the *Thomas Drayton*. D'you want their attention called to it?"

He looked back at me with that glimmer of mischief and danger in his eyes that I had often seen there before, and he said: "It might just as well be kept in the dark, partner."

I kept it in the dark. Mannock, also, knew. But he said nothing about it. The joy went out of his face, that was all, and he went about his work with a dark, thoughtful look.

Old White-Water Sam came out to see us all; he had been hearing about the preparations for the cruise, of course. He spotted one of the boys who he knew best on the deck of the ship, and he said: "Hello, Willie. Where you boys going to take that old boat?"

"Going north, Sam," said Willie.

"Going north? Going north?" murmured Sam. "Now, that's a funny thing. How in thunder you gonna get her north? On sleds or on wings?"

"With a kite," said Willie, laughing.

Sam laughed, too.

"Who was fool enough to say that we were going north?" asked one of the deck hands, standing nearby.

"Where else would we go, except on a pleasure cruise around Lake Bennett?" asked Willie.

"Yeah, and there's something in that, too," said the other fellow. "And Decatur, he don't look like there was much pleasure ahead for us."

That was true. There was a grimness in the face of Larry all the time.

White-Water said: "She's a good craft, and a true-built one. She ain't like a boat that I heard a story told about once. Her name was the *Denver Belle*, and she had a good white-water pilot . . . he started out to run her . . . ."

Said Willie loudly: "I know about that yarn, Sam. But, say, don't you think that this here boat rides too deep after?"

White-Water was put off the scent of his tale, and he stood back and looked the boat over with the eye of one who knows.

Then he said: "No, sir. I don't see nothing wrong. She rides like a gull, I'd say. You could take her out into the deep sea, if you strung up some bulwarks along the sides of her, and maybe put a keel under her. She'd roll a bit, but she'd do at sea, even. She's built to stand something, is what she's built for."

I was glad that White-Water Sam approved of the ship. And I was even gladder that Willie had put him off the trail of the tale of the *Denver Belle*. But I was gladdest of all when I saw Sam wandering back down the dock toward his saloon. Because I was afraid that he might chance to peer close through the heavy mist and see the new name that had been painted so big and fresh on the *Thomas Drayton*.

We finished our day's shifts, and Dick Wainwright, our cook, stewed up a fine mulligan, and the boys washed the mulligan down with black coffee, and turned into their bunks. They were a pretty happy lot. They weren't very much worried about what might happen to the river boat, and I suppose, with all of them together, like that, they felt pretty much at ease. There's a courage that comes out of numbers. I've heard old sailors say, even when a ship was sinking, there was a queer absence of fear if a man could stand on the deck and look around and see a lot of familiar forms and faces. I can imagine how the thing would be, too.

I turned in and slept about two hours and woke up with a start. I had had a catnap after lunch that day, to make up for the sleep I had missed when Lefty and Denny tried their dirty work on board the boat. Perhaps I was slept out now, or perhaps it was something else—I don't dare to say what, for fear of seeming superstitious—that set all my nerves jumping at once and got me up out of bed.

I walked up on deck, loading a pipe, and lighting it. Then I stood in the white, slowly lifting fog, puffing at the pipe and tasting nothing. It's hard to taste smoke when you can't see it, I've found out.

After a time I saw a strange figure, coming through the mist, that seemed to walk like a man, yet it didn't have a man's shape at all. Then, when I looked closer, I saw that it was a man, but with something big and clumsy loaded on top of his shoulders. It looked like a great sack that he was carrying.

He came up to the gangway that had been run ashore when the work of preparing the ship began. When he turned in to board us, I stepped before him and said: "Who's there?"

"Who the mischief wants to know?" asked the voice of Larry.

"Why, Larry," I said, "and what in blazes are you doing with that thing on your shoulder, whatever it is?"

Whatever it was, it seemed to weigh a lot, and Larry was puffing and blowing as he came up the gangplank.

"I'll give you a hand," I said.

"Back up and leave me alone," grunted Larry, and, getting toward the top of the gangway, he turned down the deck and disappeared down the companionway toward his own cabin.

I stared after him, with my eyes hurting, they were straining so hard, and my brain hurting, too, because it was trying to put things together.

Because, mind you, as Larry went by me, I was sure that I smelled chloroform, and smelled it good and strong.

There's nothing else in the world that I know of that has the same odor. And it's always been a rather welcome smell to me since one day a fool of a Texas mule planted both heels on my right shoulder and dislocated it so bad you'd hardly call it a shoulder at all. Well, I lay on my side groaning till a doctor came, and he clamped a cloth and a screen over my mouth, and then started to drop the chloroform on it. When I got a whiff or two of the stuff and felt it killing the pain and filling my brain full of numbness, I opened my lungs to it and it put me out like a light. When I woke up again, my arm and shoulder were plastered with bandages.

I tell you this yarn to let you know why it was that I was so sure of the whiff of chloroform that I had smelled.

Then I started to walk after Larry to ask him what he meant by shanghaiing somebody on board the boat. But I remembered a few things about Larry, and felt that perhaps it would be best not to say a word to him about it.

While I was still turning these ideas back and forth in my mind, up comes Larry to the deck, still breathing hard, and his chest heaving, and he said to me: "Joe, rouse up Mannock and turn out the crew. We're getting under way."

I started to obey and turned away from him, saying over my shoulder quietly: "Who was that you brought on board filled with chloroform, just now?"

He only stared back at me, with the flame wavering in his eyes.

"Go turn out the crew, because we're getting under way," he repeated.

XIV

You may ask if I thought that all was well in this odd proceeding, and I shall answer that I was not such a fool. But what was I to do, and how was I to make any effective protest and against what?

At any rate, I went down and turned out the crew, and, since there was already a head of steam up, we would be ready in another moment to cast off the mooring lines and proceed—where?

Well, it was such a time as comes, now and then, when a man finds his mind far too hurried for dwelling upon the future; the present totally absorbs him.

When I had started things going below, I came above and got on deck in time to see a thing that I would not willingly have missed. Through that solid wall of mist came two forms up the dock, one huge and one small, then the gigantic voice of Big Ed Graem began to bellow for Larry Decatur.

Larry was there at the rail in a minute. The gangplank already had been pulled in and Graem was calling out that it would have to be thrust out again or he would shoot down every man who attempted to cast off a mooring line. He had a double-barreled shotgun in his hands to prove his point, as it were. It did not need an advanced imagination to guess that gun was not loaded with birdshot.

Said Larry: "What's the matter with you now, Graem? I've had trouble enough with you already to suit me."

"You're going to have more trouble still," said Graem, "and you may have so much trouble that you'll never get over it. You hear me?"

"I hear you," said Larry, as calm and cool as could be.

"You've got a man on board that boat who has to come off," said Graem.

"What man is that?" asked my new boss.

"White-Water Sam," said Graem.

I realized then that it was White-Water Sam who had been brought unconscious onto the ship.

"He's not here," said Larry.

"You lie," said Graem. He brought his gun up to the ready.

"Whether I lie or not," said Larry, "if you move that shotgun another inch toward your shoulder, I'll plaster you with a half-inch slug of lead, my friend. Put down that gun or you'll get it."

And there was his Colt, resting on the rail of the boat.

He meant what he said, plainly enough. I was standing close up, and, through the mist, I could see the way his head was held, thrust forward, and I knew that another ounce of anger, in him, would pull the trigger of the revolver.

Well, what of it, when a man is threatened with a shotgun? It would be self-defense in any court in the world, I dare say.

Then, from that mist-shrouded smaller form beside Graem, came a cry. It was Nelly Bridgeman exclaiming: "Larry, don't do it! Don't fire! You've got father on board, and I must have him back!"

"The girl, too," I heard Larry mutter. "Rotten luck." He said finally: "What makes you think that your father's on board, Nelly?"

"Because I saw you go into his room. I was awake and I saw you!"

"Come on board, then," said Larry Decatur in a hard, steady voice that did one no good to hear. "Come on board and see for yourself if you're right. But leave that big hulk behind you when you come."

"I go where she goes," said Graem, standing closer to the girl.

I heard Larry curse in a whisper. Then he said: "Did you bring Ed along to force a way on board this boat, Nelly?"

"I had to have someone with me," she said.

"You couldn't trust me, eh?" Larry said bitterly.

And she answered, half sadly and half defiantly: "I thought that it would be better to have Ed Graem along."

Larry hesitated.

He was a fellow in whom any hesitation seemed a very strange thing. A moment's pause with him was a greater wonder than a year's delay in almost any other man.

At last he snapped over his shoulder at me: "Joe, get the gang-plank on shore, will you?"

I called some deck hands, and we shoved out the gangway on its wheels, and up the passage, with its canvas-filled rails, came the girl, first, and Big Ed Graem second.

When they stepped on the deck, Larry said: "You boys take Nelly down to my cabin. Nelly, you'll find there what you want.

You'll find him sleeping, but he's all right. There's no harm done to him."

She started off, almost running, with the two men showing her the way. As they turned down the companionway, Big Ed Graem seemed to come out of a trance and started to follow them.

"Here, you," snapped Larry. "You stay back here!"

"I'll see you dead first," said Graem.

"You're on my ship, and my word's law on this deck," said Larry. "Will you go on shore?"

"I'll not budge till Nelly goes with me," said Graem, "and White-Water Sam along with her. I'm going to show you the end of your rope, you fool."

"Are you?" Larry said softly.

"I am!" roared Graem, his old temper taking him and filling his throat.

"Here's something to show you an end of your own," Larry said, and, stepping in, he tapped Graem alongside of the head with the barrel of the Colt, which had flicked out into his hand again.

I heard the hollow, metal barrel ring as though it had been struck on a stone; Graem sagged at the knees and slipped down to his hands. The shotgun, falling too, toppled over the side, slipped under the rail, and splashed into the water.

Larry turned on me and handed me the gun.

"Take this big fool below and lock him in a cabin," he said. "And if he makes any trouble on the way, shoot him full of lead."

I did what was told me. It was impossible for me, I don't know why, to oppose the will of Larry Decatur just then. Larry helped that more than half stunned man to his feet, and Graem, muttering, staggering, all at sea, only had sense enough to realize that the muzzle of a gun was between his ribs and that he was getting his marching orders.

What should I have done if he had come to, fully, and started struggling? Well, certainly I should never have pulled the trigger, but I might have clubbed that big head with the weight of the gun.

There was no need. Graem was only recovered enough to hold a hand to his head and curse as I pushed him into a cabin and locked the door on him.

That door seemed a flimsy barrier against the burly shoulders of the giant, but at least I had obeyed orders.

Then I came on deck, and saw the lines being taken off the mooring posts along the dock.

The news of what was happening had traveled along shore, and through the fog I saw many forms, dimly appearing, all shouting and calling out to one another.

Jay Weston, an old river man, was in the pilot house, and Steve Mannock was in the engine room. We were pretty well equipped to handle the *Thomas Drayton*—or the *Denver Belle*, to give her new name.

Now a bell chimed twice, and the engines, in reverse, began to pound with a long, easy rhythm, and the paddle wheel churned the water, splashing the paddles with a great slapping against the face of the lake. So we pulled out and back from the dock, and far off, losing sight of the shore. Then her nose turned downstream.

Beside the entrance to the pilot house, I found Larry Decatur. The shouting and the cheering still came to us from the unseen shore, along with laugher at this foolish, blind adventure. But these sounds were momently growing fainter, as I said to Larry: "Why didn't you put Ed Graem on shore?"

"He might have come to before we got the boat away," said Larry. "Besides, he's tangled himself up in whatever fate lies ahead for me, the boat, and Nelly, and White-Water. I can feel that in my blood and bones."

I said nothing. The pulse of my blood was a sickening hammer stroke in my temples. I've never felt as I felt then. Heaven forbid that I ever should again.

He said: "Be useful, Joe. There are some things, just now, that only you can help me with."

"How can I help you," I asked, "unless I know where you're taking the boat?"

"I'm taking her to the upper mouth of Miles Cañon," he said. "Now you know that much. Go below to my cabin, and see what's happening there. Say anything that comes into your head."

I went down to the cabin, not at all wanting to be there, and, when I went in, I found that old White-Water was just opening his eyes, and Nelly, white-faced, her eyes swollen with tears, was bathing his head with cold water.

She turned her head and looked at me. "What's happening?" she said.

I answered frankly: "We're going down to the head of Miles Cañon. I don't know what's the matter with Larry. He must be crazy. I never heard of a man acting the way that he's doing."

"He's not crazy," she said. "He means what he says. He has something in his mind."

I thought that there was something strange in that remark.

"Can I help?" I said.

"You can't help," she said. "Not here. I'll take care of Father. Go back on deck and be useful for Larry, if you can. I've an idea that he needs help, now, more than he ever needed it before in his life."

Mind you, this was the way that she talked about a man who had drugged and kidnapped her father!

Well, I saw the explanation at a glance. She loved that vagabond of a lazy tramp, Decatur. She loved him so much that she could not criticize his actions.

XV

We ran down to the head of Miles Cañon, and two different things happened on the way.

The first was when big Graem smashed down the door that held him and came raging onto the deck. Larry, his revolver and the white bull terrier, Docile, met him.

Larry said: "You're going to get a chance to get off this boat before long, if you want to. But as long as you stay on board, if you lift a hand to make trouble of any kind, I'll kill you, Graem."

There was no misunderstanding that sort of talk.

Graem looked at him with a sort of baffled savagery in his eyes, and nodded. "You've got me again, for the time being," he said. "But the end of the game hasn't come."

"That's all right," said Larry. "But your part of it will have to be played out on shore."

That was the end of Graem for the time being.

The other thing that happened was when White-Water Sam came on deck, not half an hour before we arrived just above the cañon.

He strolled about the deck with Nelly, laughing and happy, hailing me and Larry, and apparently not realizing in the least how he came aboard the ship, but very glad to be there.

Nelly showed the effects of the strain, but she tried to smile. I went forward with them, when Sam insisted on leaning over the rail and watching the bow waves rising and come hissing back from the cut water.

There he leaned, and then recovered himself with a wild cry. He turned about on us with staring, terrible eyes, and shouted: "She's the *Denver Belle!* She's the *Denver Belle!*"

He'd seen the name painted there by Larry, of course. I had forgotten about that.

Nelly gripped his arm and started talking to him, but he shook his head at her. I never saw such a baffled look as that which came in his eyes.

He said: "But I thought the *Denver Belle* . . . I thought . . . I mean, I heard a story about her. And the story was about a slick pilot, a regular white-water man, that decided to run her . . . ."

He broke off as the voice of Larry broke in on us. He had come forward, and he was as calm as could be, the rascal. He said: "People are always making up names. But this is the real *Denver Belle*. There's no other *Denver Belle* than this one."

"But I thought . . ." said old Sam.

"You had a dream about her, maybe," said Larry. "People are always having dreams, and then getting them mixed up with real daylight."

"A dream?" Sam said slowly. "A dream? Yes, maybe it was a bad dream. I've got to sit down and think."

He did as he said, sitting down in a corner on a stool, with his eyes straining far away into time, trying to see something. Nelly sat beside him, still as stone, watching his tormented face.

I said to Larry: "What d'you mean by it?"

"I don't know," said Larry, shaking his head. "It's an idea. I may be wrong, but I'm going to try it."

I knew better than to ask him what the idea was. I could see by the look of him that he was already in a torment of doubt and of pain.

We came close up to the mouth of the cañon, so close that the roaring of the water came to us out of the mouth of the gorge, so close that the powerful current began to suck at us, and we had to put the paddle wheel full steam astern in order to get up to the bank and tie up. The bow kept wavering out toward the center of the current, and being knocked back again, and the mooring rope groaned with the strain that was put on it.

Then, with everybody on deck, Larry said to us, just loud enough for everyone to hear: "Boys, I'm going to run the cañon, and the White Horse Rapids. If any of you'll stay with me, good. If you won't, I'll pilot her through myself, or try to. I suppose that most of you will want to go ashore. You're welcome to."

Go ashore? Of course, they wanted to go ashore. From the pilot down, the whole lot cleaned out at once, and left only Steve Mannock and me on board. And there was Nelly and her father, and Graem trying to get the old man to follow onto the safe land.

But old man Bridgeman kept shaking his head.

"There's something about it. It ain't all a dream," he said. "Seems to me like there was once a *Denver Belle*, and I was the pilot of her, and there was men . . . ."

He stared wildly about him and shook his head again.

Then Larry said: "Graem, here's a chance for you to do something. Will you take Nelly on shore, please? Then we'll get her father to follow her."

Graem suddenly pointed a finger at Larry and cursed him.

"I see through the scheme, now," he said. "You want to get White-Water Sam to pilot you through. You murdering sneak, that's your idea."

I had guessed at the thing before. But I was surprised by the voice of Mannock at my shoulder, saying: "And maybe the old boy could do it. He's lived through Miles Cañon once without a boat under him . . . maybe he could take the second boat straight through." He added: "I'm going to stay and see it through."

"You're a fool . . . you're chucking yourself away," I said.

"And what about you?" he said.

"I've sort of got to stay with the ship and Larry," I said, for I felt that way—sick with fear, but tied to the job.

Larry was saying: "He's right. White-Water, you're the best river pilot in Alaska. This is your boat to take through the cañon, and you can do it. If you want to go up there in the pilot house, you're the boss. Will you go?"

"Why, where else would I go?" said White-Water Sam. "I'm the pilot on the *Denver Belle*, ain't I? And this is the *Denver Belle*, ain't it? I'll have full steam up, Larry."

And he turned and started to climb to the top deck.

Graem would have gone after him, with the cry of Nelly Bridgeman in his ear, but Larry and his gun stopped the try.

"You go back and get Nelly on shore," said Larry. "You can't have Sam."

Graem roared out like a bull. He left Nelly standing, dazed and helpless, and, running to the rear of the boat, he called out: "Boys, Decatur has gone mad! He's going to try to run the cañon and the White Horse with poor old Sam for a pilot. Will you come aboard and help me to get Sam off?"

Would they come? You bet they would come, and boiling. I never saw men so hot and angry. Then, as Larry saw them start on board, he knew that there was only one trick left for him to play. He swung a double-bitted axe, and, with one blow, he cut the mooring line so deep that the pull of the current did the rest. The cable parted with a pop like the explosion of a gun, and the new *Denver Belle* shot well out into the current.

XVI

There was no gun in the hand of Larry now and, with only the axe against him, I think Graem would have rushed straight in and taken his chances of killing or of being killed, but he was able to hear the cry of Nelly, as she called: "Ed, Ed! There's nothing to be done, but all help. We're lost unless we all pull together!"

There was sense enough in that.

The current was swinging the ship around and sweeping it down the stream, broadside on, to wedge at the mouth of Miles Cañon. From the pilot house, old White-Water Sam was ringing vain orders, because there was no one, for the moment, in the engine room. But Mannock was there the next moment, yelling as he went below: "One of you get to the fires. I'll handle the engines!"

It was Graem who did the firing on that run. Mannock handled the engines and handled them wonderfully well. The pilot was White-Water Sam. The deck crew was composed of Larry Decatur, who had thrown us all down at death's door, and Nelly and me.

But what was a deck crew to do?

We were picking up and now we flung forward. The churning wheel and the rudder, pulled clear over, barely straightened her out so that her bow hit the opening of the channel in the center.

Nothing could help us now, nothing except the hands and the brain of the old man in the pilot house.

We saw him leaning out, and there was on his face the same look that I had seen before in the saloon, when he was talking about the run of the first *Denver Belle*. He was smiling, I mean to say, and he was looking down on that shooting flume of water as though it were the still water of a harbor, a home harbor, after a long, long voyage.

Mind you, that was the poor madman who we had all pitied so, and now Larry Decatur had cast us all into the hollow of his hand. The least faltering, and we were gone!

Two hundred men had died, trying to shoot through the cañon and the White Horse Rapids beyond. Two hundred men! Not on steamers, mind you, but in small boats that could be handed through with ropes, now and then, in tight places. But even they, no matter how built and how handled, could not always get through. Two hundred men had been beaten by that water, and it was ready to eat as many more.

Have you ever seen the Miles Cañon?

Imagine rock walls, standing up straight and flat as the palm of your hand, sometimes two hundred feet high, with a dark fringing of evergreens along the tops. Imagine between those walls a gorge only eighty feet wide; only eighty feet wide, and yet containing the whole flow of a great river!

How could such a narrow gap hold the water? It never could in the world, except that the descent is so sharp that the water goes hurling through faster than you'd believe. Like running horses it flows, and the fury of the current piles it in a foaming, shuddering ridge in the center, away from the walls on each side.

That was the task of White-Water Sam, to ride the exact center of that ridge of boiling water; if the prow slipped off even a yard or so, we were almost sure to swing broadside on, just exactly as the first *Denver Belle* had done. In that case, a miracle had enabled one life to be saved; two such miracles could never happen.

I stood out there on the prow for a minute, but I could not stand it, with the whole body of the ship trembling under me, the keel sliding this way and that, and the kick of the rudder as plainly felt, now and then, as a slap on the face.

I went back and climbed to the pilot house, and there were Larry and the girl, she standing behind her father at the wheel, her hands folded behind her back and pressing against the wall; on her face, strangely enough, just the same expression that was in the face of her father.

I mean to say, there was a sort of brooding and mysterious content in her look, and there was the same thing in the face of White-Water Sam.

She was not looking that way for the same reason. He was once more back in his element, steering a ship through white water. That was why he looked like a dreaming artist, as he steadied the keel on the ridge of the churning, leaping water.

But she? Well, she was making a voyage through some region of the mind.

And then I saw a strange thing. It was Larry Decatur, never giving a glance to his ship, but keeping his eyes steadily riveted on the face of the old pilot.

It was as though he could see in that face a reflection of all the dangers that were rushing before them down the stream. But he was doing more than that.

He was looking upon the face of White-Water, I tell you, not so much in the hope that the old fellow could bring them through, but with a sort of half-devout and half-childish hope that White-Water Sam himself might arrive at some great goal before that river run was ended.

I had rather liked Larry for a long time, but I had always suspected him a good deal, and put him down for a fox, which no doubt he was, in part. But now my suspicion and my distrust all vanished, for it was pretty plain to see what he meant by this experiment.

He might get the new *Denver Belle* through the cañon. Yes, there was that possibility. But there was another possibility. I could not help remembering what he had said about the fellow who feared snakes, until he was bitten a second time.

Yes, that must be the great idea that had come into the wild brain of Larry, and now he was putting it to the test. That, in the testing, he should risk five lives, including his own, besides the life of old White-Water himself—well, that was simply part of the character of Larry Decatur.

And now, forgetful of himself, the ship, and the girl, he studied the face of Sam Bridgeman and seemed striving to read his soul. A sort of grim joy—yes, that was what I would call the expression of Larry Decatur as he watched the pilot.

That little tableau inside the pilot house was enough for me. Nobody cared about the progress of the new *Denver Belle*, except the pilot himself and me.

But was I watching?

I tell you, a combination of a city on fire, a prize fight, and a three-ringed circus was nothing compared to the shooting of that boat down through the cañon, with the walls running by and blurred.

We seemed to be gathering speed all the time. I don't suppose that we were, but it seemed so to me, as though the old boat were getting a better hold of the water, gaining and gaining, until I found myself down on my knees, braced, with a strong grip on the rail, with the wind shooting back into my face as it shoots and tears when you're on the back of a running horse.

And the breath went out of me. It seemed to me that death was running toward us, and we were running toward it.

I caught myself shouting, with words that the wind blurred together: "Reverse the engines! Reverse the engines!"

Nobody heard me, I hope.

Then the low mouth of the cañon leaped away behind us.

Great Scott, I didn't believe it! It was like a dream to see that we were safe and sure through that mile-long flume!

I heard a tingling cry above me and looked up, and there was old White-Water Sam leaning out from the pilot house for a moment to take a side shot with his eyes down at the course before him, laughing and crying out with joy because of what he had done.

I felt a stab of joy, too, because I felt then that Larry Decatur must have accomplished what he had set out to do. We might all die. We might all be broken up in the White Horse, but one among the dead would not be a madman. He would be as sane as ever in all his days.

Now, if I tell you that the fear dropped away from me and that suddenly I forgot my miserable, selfish soul and was able to be glad in this miracle of White-Water Sam, I hope that I'll be believed, and that I'll be believed when I say that as we hit the White Horse Rapids, I was not afraid.

It's the truth.

Those rapids are well named, for the water leaps in them like wild white horses, dashing together, flinging up their manes, and thundering like all the cavalry of all the armies of the world.

Through that white mist of spray I saw a rock loom like a gigantic spear, held ready to rip us open from head to heel. Then a bell rang, and the engines backed with all their might.

We seemed to be hurling down on the rock broadside. But no, with wonderful delicacy and sureness, White-Water Sam flanked that rock, and down we shot into the currents and the dashing water beyond. Beyond that, like people stepping through a nightmare into the beautiful peace of a sunny morning, we came out into the still waters below.

We were through; we were safe. Voices came to us from the shore, and I saw dancing, wildly gesticulating men, prancing up and down and yelling their heads off.

I looked at them as Columbus or one of his crew might have looked upon the savages of the unknown shore. For those men might have been far and done much, but they never had traversed the swift and arrowy maëlstrom through which I had just gone.

I started to go up to the pilot house again, but, when I heard Nelly crying, and the steady, strong, reassuring voice of her father comforting her, I judged that it would be better to keep away.

Going aft, I saw that Big Ed Graem had come up from below and was standing with his arms folded, his face turned toward the white dashing of the rapids above us.

I did not feel that he had failed, because he had had a hand in the accomplishment of a great undertaking. But I knew the bitterness of his heart and pitied him.

The voice of Larry called my name happily from the pilot house. I hardly wanted to go to join that noisy, laughing, weeping party. But something compelled me, and I went.

Black Thunder

The year 1933 was a prolific one for Frederick Faust with twenty-seven short novels and thirteen serials being published. "Black Thunder" appeared in the July issue of *Dime Western* under his Max Brand byline. It was one of three stories to appear in the publication that year as Faust began to branch out from Street & Smith's *Western Story Magazine* once his word rate was decreased, first from 5¢ to 4¢, then to 3¢. It is both a pursuit story and a love triangle as two prospectors vie for the woman they both love.

I

The stone was quartzite and the drill was dull—yet Harrigan sank the hole rapidly, swinging the twelve-pound hammer in a sort of fury.

The hillside was a burning furnace of noonday heat—yet Harrigan would not abate his labor.

The sweat blackened the back of his flannel shirt in an irregular pattern that was water-marked with salt at the edges. That back rose and fell a little with every stroke. The shoulders worked. Two mighty, elastic ropes of muscle sprang up from the waist and spread powerful fingers across the shoulder blades. But in spite of the strength of this man, one could not help expecting him to weaken and seek rest.

Yet he did not rest. He continued steadily at his labor. An inexhaustible fuel, in fact, was being fed into the furnace of this man's strength, and the fuel was anger.

It was not merely the heat of the sun or of his labor that kept the face of Dan Harrigan red. It was not the effort of his labor that made his blue eyes gleam. It was a steady passion of anger that set his jaws and lighted his eyes from a fire of the soul. Rage was to him like a sustaining food.

A mule brayed in the valley, and Harrigan leaped to his feet. He looked down toward the water hole in high hopes. But those hopes vanished. It was not MacTee, returning at last from town. Their mule was a piebald brute, and this was the usual dust-covered beast of burden, with a man on its back. The rider, plainly not MacTee, had just left the water hole, and was heading his mount up the half-mile grade toward the mine.

Harrigan pondered this. For twenty-four hours, MacTee had been due back from town, with supplies. Yet he had not come. What, then, had happened? Had he fallen into a brawl in the town? Had the dark passions of his Scot nature boiled up until a .45-caliber bullet quieted them forever? Had that great soul, that stark and terrible spirit vanished from the earth?

Harrigan was stunned by the mere suspicion that such a thing might be. He looked up at the sky, which was pale with the flood of the sunlight, and told himself that, if MacTee had died, those heavens would be overcast by thunderheads. There would have been a sign of some sort even in the middle of the night. Lightning and sounds of doom would have accompanied the passing of MacTee.

And yet what could this be but a messenger to tell him of MacTee? What else would bring a man into the white heat of this desert? Not even buzzards wheeled in the air above the waste. Only the partnership of a MacTee and a Harrigan could have produced enough vital energy to drive men out here prospecting for gold. For two months they had broken ground, hoping that a thin vein of ore would widen. It had been bitterly hard, but Harrigan and MacTee were used to bitter hardships. They were, in fact, used to one another.

The mule came nodding up the slope. The rider had bent his head. His hands were folded on the pommel of the saddle. He would be terribly thirsty. Harrigan turned with a sigh and contemplated the jug wrapped in sacking that was placed in a shadowy nook where the wind would strike it.

The man came nearer. The bristles on his unshaven face glinted in the sun. He was as big as MacTee, Harrigan decided. He carried a rifle in a long saddle holster. There was a gun belt strapped about his hips. A big canteen bumped against the front of the saddle.

That was good. At least, he carried his own water with him.

Now he pulled up the mule close by the mine and dismounted. He looked young in years but old in the West. He stood still for a moment, staring at Harrigan, and the waves of heat rose with a dull shimmering from his sombrero. He was as lean as a desert wolf, all skin and bones and sheer power.

"Howdy," he said. "This is about the middle of hell, ain't it?"

"Yeah," said Harrigan. "This is the corner of Main Street and First Avenue, in the center of hell. You couldn't be wrong."

"All right," said the stranger. "Then you're Harrigan."

"Yes. I'm Harrigan."

"If you're Harrigan, where's MacTee?"

"He's not here," said Harrigan.

"You lie," said the man of the guns.

Suddenly Harrigan straightened. He seemed to grow younger. A tender light came into his eyes.

"Brother," he said, in the softest of voices, "did you call me a liar?"

"I asked for MacTee, and you say that he ain't here," protested the other. "If he ain't here, where is he?"

"He's in Dunphyville, yonder."

"You lie again," said the stranger. "There ain't hardly enough left of Dunphyville to cover a prairie dog. If a jack rabbit tried to hide behind what's left of Dunphyville, his ears would stick up behind the heap."

"That's twice in a row that I've been a liar," counted Harrigan, rubbing his hands together and looking rather wistfully into the face of the newcomer. "What's your name?"

"Rollo Quay," said the big man.

"Rollo," said Harrigan, "it's a funny name. It ain't the only funny thing about you, neither. But before I make you funnier, I want to find out what happened to Dunphyville."

"It was wrecked," said Quay.

"I don't know how God, man, or the devil could want to waste time to wreck that dump," said Harrigan.

"It wasn't God, man, or devil that wrecked the place. It was MacTee," said Quay.

Harrigan nodded. "MacTee got restless, did he?" said Harrigan. "Well, if he got careless and stubbed his toe on a place like Dunphyville, I guess there's not much left of the town."

"There ain't gonna be much left of MacTee, when I find him," said Quay. "Not when I meet him, there ain't gonna. I'm gonna take payment out of his black hide for everything he did to my saloon back there in Dunphyville."

"Brother," said Harrigan, "I hear you talk, and I'd certainly like to save you till you had a chance to meet him. But I don't think that I can wait that long. What was the last seen of MacTee in Dunphyville?"

"The last seen of him," said Quay, "was a cloud of dust with a streak of lightnin' through it. Nobody knows exactly where it landed. And nobody knows exactly where it disappeared to. But before I talk about Black MacTee any more, I'm gonna do something to make Red Harrigan a little bit redder. You Irish son of a hoop snake and a bobtailed lynx, I'm gonna take you apart, first, and find out where that skunk of a MacTee is, later on."

He stepped straight forward, feinted in workman-like manner with his left, and drove an excellent right for the head.

Harrigan ducked his head half an inch and shed that punch as a rock sheds water.

"Here's the same sock with a hook to it," said Harrigan, and knocked Mr. Quay under the hoofs of the mule.

Rollo Quay sat up half a minute later and laid one hand on the side of his jaw. Then he saw that Harrigan was sitting on the back of the mule. The revolvers that Quay reached for were gone.

"I'll leave the mule in Dunphyville, safe and sound," said Harrigan.

"Damn the mule," said Quay. "What I want to know is . . . where did you hide that blackjack when your sleeves was turned up to the elbow?"

"That was no blackjack. That was the hook in the end of that punch," said Harrigan. "I'm going to look for MacTee. If he happens to drop in here while I'm gone, talk soft and low to him, brother. I'm only a sort of chore boy around here. But Black MacTee is a man."

II

There were only a dozen buildings in Dunphyville but they all seemed in place to the eye of Harrigan, as he drew near the town. In spite of the storm of which Quay had spoken, nothing appeared wrong, until Harrigan entered the single street.

Then he noted sundry details of interest. Most of the windows were broken. The chairs on the front verandah of the hotel were missing one leg or two, and several of them had been converted into stools. All the Es in the sign General Merchandise Store had disappeared and were represented by ragged eyeholes of light. And the whole side of the blacksmith shop was scorched and the ground blackened beside it, as though the dead grass had been kindled in an effort to burn the town.

Harrigan stopped the mule in front of the saloon. The two swinging doors were gone. The two front windows were smashed out. Broken glass glittered in the dust of the street. One of the frail wooden pillars that held up the roof over the verandah was broken in the middle and sagged to the side. The darkness inside had about it an empty air of desolation.

"Yes," murmured Harrigan, "it looks like Black MacTee."

He dismounted from the mule, made comfortable the revolver that was under his coat, and entered the saloon through the open doorway.

It was indeed an empty spot.

Of the long mirror that had reflected so many sun-burned faces, there remained against the wall only a few shreds of brightness and gilding. Of the long array of bottles whose necks and brilliant labels had shone on the shelf behind the bar, all were gone except half a dozen lonely last survivors. The brass rail was bent and broken from its brackets. Bullets had ripped the polished surface of the bar itself. And behind the bar leaned the one time stalwart figure of a fat man in a dirty apron. He wore a plaster over one cheek, a leather patch over one eye, a red-stained bandage around his head, and his left arm was supported in a sling.

"Hello," said Harrigan. "What happened?"

The barman looked toward Harrigan with one dull eye.

"Hullo," he said in a hollow voice. "There was a kind of an explosion. After that, I don't seem to remember nothin' very clear."

"Let's have a drink," said Harrigan, putting one elbow on the splintered edge of the bar.

"There ain't nothing to drink except brandy at a dollar a throw," said the barman. "All the rest . . . ." He made a vague gesture with one hand. He turned to follow his own gesture and survey the destruction.

"We'll have the brandy, then," said Harrigan.

The barman found one of the few bottles that remained and set it with a glass before Harrigan.

"You're drinking, too," said Harrigan.

The barman filled a glass for himself, sadly.

"Now," said Harrigan. "What happened the other day when Black MacTee was here?"

"It all started right over there in the corner," said the barman. "MacTee was loaded up to start for his mine. His mule was hitched outside the door. And MacTee was settin' there in the corner, readin' a stack of the old newspapers that we keep there. There was a dozen of the boys in here, most of them from the Curley Ranch." He paused, re-filled his brandy glass by sense of touch while his eyes still contemplated the memory. "All I recollect after that," said the barman, "ain't very much. I remember that MacTee come over here to the bar and set 'em up all around for the boys. They all drank, and he set 'em up again. And then he lifted up his whiskey glass and he hollered out . . . 'To Kate, boys . . . .'"

"My God," said Harrigan. "What was it he said? To Kate? What put him on that track? What newspaper was he reading? Tell me, man . . . what newspaper was he reading?"

The flame of his hair was the flame of his eyes. He devoured the very soul of the man before him.

"Wait a minute. Don't hurry me or I'm gonna have a relapse," said the bartender. "He ups with his glass and says . . . 'To Kate.' And everybody hollers out and downs the drink, except me. And when he sees that my glass is still full, he says what's the matter with me, and I say no disrespect to the Kate that he knows, but that once I got tangled up with a freckle-faced snake by that name, and, ever since, when I heard the name of Kate, I got shootin' pains and colic. Well, I no sooner says that, than he reaches across the bar and slams me, and I drop off into a deep sleep. When I wake up, this here is what I see."

"Kate," said Harrigan. "He's spotted her. He's gone. For the love of the dear God, tell me, man, where's the newspaper that he was reading when he let out that Indian yell?"

"Where's the beer gone, and the soda, and the bar whiskey, and . . .?"

"Shut up," said Harrigan.

And the barman was silent, for he found in the eye of Harrigan something that was hard to meet. The blank fury of the great MacTee was not as terrible as the blue lightning that was now in the eyes of Harrigan.

"How far to the railroad?" demanded Harrigan.

"Seven miles," gasped the barman.

"Tell Quay, when he comes back, that his mule will be over at the railroad. So long."

And Harrigan fled through the doorway and leaped into the saddle on the mule's back.

III

The town of Caldwell Junction contained not a great many more buildings than Dunphyville, outside of the railroad station and the sheds. In such a small town it was not surprising, therefore, that the first thing Harrigan saw was the pinto mule with the black and white tail, standing outside of the grocery store. The grocer himself was loading a wicker basket, filled with supplies, into a cart to which the mule was hitched.

"Where'd you get the mule?" asked Harrigan.

The grocer was pink and white. All grocers have that complexion. His pink turned to red, and his white turned to pink, when he faced Harrigan.

"There was a man here the other day," he said.

"Big . . . black hair . . . drunk . . . happy?" asked Harrigan.

"Yes," said the grocer. "What has he done? Are you after him? Who is he?"

"He's a double-crossing Scotch black-souled hound," said Harrigan. "Did you buy this mule from him?"

"Yes," said the grocer, shrinking from the red and blue flame of Harrigan.

Harrigan groaned—in his mind's eye was the haunting picture of a lovely girl whose given name was Kate.

"The big man with the black eyes, he pulled out of this town on a train, I don't doubt. What train was it?"

"It was headed south. It was a freight," said the grocer, rather frightened.

"What train is this one?" asked Harrigan suddenly, as a whistle shrieked up the track.

"That's the Overland, bound south," said the grocer.

"Then it doesn't stop here?"

"No. It just takes the grade slow, and . . . ."

But Harrigan, without waiting to hear more, without waiting for the money that had been promised, turned and sprinted down the street. He saw the engine's head come nobly into view, swaying with speed. He saw that speed quenched somewhat by the upgrade passing the Junction. But still the train was thundering along, dust and cinders whipping under its wheels as it shot by the station.

Harrigan, turning with it as the tender went by, sprinted with all his might. He reached his full speed as the observation car went past and he leaped high and far for the iron balustrade that fenced in the rear platform.

He caught with both hands. The grip of one was broken. For an instant his body streamed out behind the flying train. Then he drew himself lightly up and scrambled aboard.

The conductor came on the run, half a minute later. He took Harrigan by the collar. "Bums like you oughta die," said the conductor. "I've a mind to throw you off now. If we weren't behind time, I'd stop the train on the trestle, and heave you off into the gulch. But when we hit the next stop, you'll be on your way to jail, young fellow."

Said Harrigan: "You're mistaking me, my friend. My brother-in-law, Mister Peter Van Houston Dyce, is on board this train. I had to ride fifty miles to get here to tell him that his father has just been roughed up by a bear on my ranch."

"Get out of this observation car and stand on the front platform, you lying bum," said the conductor.

So Harrigan stood for eighty miles on the front platform, and smiled as he heard the roar of the wheels and their rapid syncopation over the tracks.

It was nearing dusk when they reached the next stop. Harrigan slid off on the blind side of the train, and walked ahead as far as the first signal light. When the train passed that point, gathering speed, it gathered Harrigan, also, into its blind baggage.

The vigilance of the conductor, who was led by a spirit of eerie inquiry, found Harrigan on the blind baggage, fifty miles farther south. He tried to brain Harrigan with a signal lantern, but the red-headed man escaped. He rode another seventy miles on the tops of the coaches, or between them, but at the last he was driven from this refuge.

The whole train crew, by this time, had sharpened its eyes, hardened its fists, and roused its soul for this contest with a daring tramp. But it was not until the gray of the dawn that Harrigan, after haunting that express all through the night, at last, left the Overland. He would not have left it even then, except that he began to feel that perhaps he had overstepped his proper distance south. Therefore, in fear that Black MacTee might have ceased traveling in this direction, he dropped off at the railroad yards of a big cattle-shipping town to look about him and make inquiry.

Three railroad detectives closed suddenly on him like three little kingbirds on one big hawk. He did not run. He did not fight. He let two of them hold him by the arms while the third rammed the muzzle of a revolver into the pit of his stomach.

"You're Harrigan," said the third man.

"With that gun in front of you, you can call me worse things than that," said Harrigan.

"It's a big rap that you've got to stand for," said the detective.

"What's the charge against me," asked Harrigan, "and who made it?"

"You murdered Joe Chantry, up yonder," said the man who carried the gun. "And the gent that told us about you is the man that you're chasing south. He's the next one that you want to bump off. He didn't look like the sort of a bird who'd run away, neither."

Harrigan blinked.

"As big as me, or bigger?" he asked. "Black hair and black eyes and a dark skin?"

"Yes," said the man with the gun. "Come along, Harrigan. He warned us that you're likely to make trouble. But the first trouble you start with us is gonna break your back and split your wishbone. Understand?"

"I understand," said Harrigan, "that he'd have me hanged to get me off his trail, and be damned to him. It's Black MacTee, and gone blacker than ever. Oh, yes, I understand. I never heard of a man called Joe Chantry . . . but I understand."

He was marching forward with a man on either arm, and the man with the gun behind him. Now he stumbled, or seemed to stumble, and kicked out behind him with the fine precision of an Army mule. The gun carrier shot a hole in the morning sky and went down with a pair of battered shins. Harrigan threw the other two detectives on top of him, collected three guns, and ran toward the rumbling sound of a long freight that was pulling out on the southern route.

It was a train of empties. He hooked his ride, found a boxcar, and slipped through the open door. On the floor he sat while the dust danced on the trembling boards and the landscape swept by him. Mountains near and far, then a series of black tunnels, with open country beyond, a smiling land of rolling hills with groves of trees shading it, and the flash of water running in every valley.

They passed the scattered houses of another large cow town. As the train slowed, Harrigan left two of the revolvers in the boxcar and swung down to the ground. He had to sprint hard, because the train was still traveling fast. And while he was still helpless with the speed of his running, trying to keep from pitching forward on his face, leaning back his head and shoulders, he saw a long, lean man, with a deep-visored cap pulled well over his eyes, come out from behind one of the piles of ties that were corded here at the end of the railroad yard.

This man raised a hand with the bright flash of a gun in it. Harrigan had been running as fast as he could, before this. He tried now to increase his speed. The end of the freight train went by with a departing thunder. He heard the voice of the man with the gun shouting for him to stop. A gun barked. But Harrigan dived the next instant around the corner of one of the big stacks of ties.

There he waited. He looked down at his shoulder and saw the glint of bare skin. The bullet had nipped away a bit of the strong flannel cloth.

Footfalls rushed up, crunching on cinders. A shadow sloped over the ground around the corner of the ties. So Harrigan sprang at that instant and laid the barrel of the gun he had kept along the head of the pursuer.

Afterward he sat the limp body on the ground and waited for life to return to the eyes. He picked up the man's fallen revolver. Inside the coat of the man he found the shield of a railroad detective. Up the sleeve of the coat, he found a handy blackjack.

His victim groaned. Harrigan took the man by his long chin and shook his head violently.

"Brother," said Harrigan, looking down into the bright, dangerous eyes, "you're another that MacTee has made a fool of. He's told you to look out for Harrigan. He's told you that Harrigan is wanted for the killing of a fellow named Chantry. Well, boy, I never heard of a gent named Chantry and that's a fact. But I've heard of Black MacTee. Where is he? Which way did he go? Further south?"

The bright little eyes looked at Harrigan without expression. They were simply bright.

"All right," said Harrigan. "I hate to do it, but I'm fighting against time."

He took the hand of the detective, pulled his arm rigid, and then tapped him with the blackjack across the ridge of the tight shoulder muscles.

The detective closed his eyes and turned gray-green. Harrigan took the other arm, jerked it tight, brought down the blackjack on a similar spot.

"All right," said the detective. "That's enough." His eyes opened again. "Why not?" he said. "I don't know what the game is that you two thugs are playing, but I know that I want you to meet. He left the railroad line, right here. I dunno where he faded to."

Harrigan went to a barbershop for a shave. The barber was so fat that even the effort of standing made him pant a little.

"I read something in the paper, a while ago," Harrigan remarked, deciding to try a shot in the dark. "The news came from here. It was about a girl with an Irish name. Her name is Kate Malone . . . ."

"She ain't from here," said the barber. "You mean the schoolteacher that saved her pupils when the school caught on fire?"

"That's the one," said Harrigan.

"She ain't from here," said the barber. "She's teaching a crossroads school, eight miles out on the Cullen Road."

Harrigan left the shop and went to a clothing store. He bought a necktie and a cheap coat, then found the Cullen Road. A buckboard drew up from behind, stopped, took him in without a word. The driver was a grim-faced rancher who kept looking straight before him and never spoke.

"I'm trying to locate my sister, Kate Malone," said Harrigan.

The rancher turned his head a little, but looked at the distance, instead of at Harrigan.

"I reckon that she's found a whole crop of brothers, since the school burned down," he said.

He spoke no more for an hour. The green hills drifted slowly behind them while the two mustangs dog-trotted sullenly along, heads down, enduring the miles.

At last, the old rancher pulled up the team and pointed to a cluster of trees around a red roof.

"That's the Tyndale house," he said. "That's where Kate Malone is living while the school's rebuilding. I hope she remembers your face, young man."

161

IV

There was a pleasant wind that tumbled a few white clouds across the sky. The hills were the finest Harrigan ever had seen. Never had there been such cattle as those that dotted the wide range. The very air was different, for Kate Malone also was breathing it.

He went up the side lane, opened the gate, and passed on to the house. A Negro in a cook's apron was carrying stove wood from the woodshed toward the kitchen door. Down the slope behind the house Harrigan saw, through the tree trunks, the gleam of running water.

"I'm looking for Angus MacTee," said Harrigan.

"Yes, sir," said the cook. "I guess he ain't here, sir."

"No?" said Harrigan. "Is Miss Kate Malone here, then?"

"No, sir, I guess she ain't here, neither." The cook rolled his eyes. "She was called away, sir," he said, "by a message from town, and . . . ."

Harrigan grinned suddenly.

"How much did MacTee pay you for telling me that lie?" he asked. "Ten dollars?"

"No, sir. Five dollars," said the cook. "I mean . . . ." He stopped short, his thick lips parted, his eyes perfectly rounded as he saw that he had been so easily trapped.

"Is MacTee here now?" asked Harrigan.

"He . . . be . . ." stammered the cook. "I guess so."

"Is he down there by the creek? Is he with her?" asked Harrigan, pointing.

The cook was silent, agape. So Harrigan marched straight down the hill, through the heat of the sun and the cool touch of the shadows, until he came close to the edge of the water. Then he heard voices, and slipped from tree to tree until he could see Kate Malone herself sitting on a rock at the side of the stream. The current curved toward the other bank, at this point, and in the still eddy lay the image of the girl with a patch of sun in her hair. Black Angus MacTee stood beside her.

Since she was turned away from him, somewhat, MacTee did not need to guard his facial expression. Under the great dark ridges of his brows, his eyes burned with a black fire.

When Harrigan saw the man, it seemed to him that he was dwarfed by the dimensions of MacTee and by the pride and furious, headlong desire in the face of the man.

"What I want to know is not much, Kate," said Angus MacTee. "It's only to find out if you mind me being here close to you. It's only to find out if you care the least mite for me, Kate."

She looked up, not at MacTee, but at the long, bright slope of the hill beyond the creek.

"I've owed my life to you, Angus," said the girl. "How could I help caring for you? Except for you and Dan Harrigan . . . ."

"Poor Harrigan," said MacTee. "There was a man."

The girl got up from her place and looked straight into the face of MacTee. And Harrigan would have given worlds to have been standing nearer to study her expression.

"Is Dan Harrigan dead?" she asked. Her voice was level. Who could tell what emotion was behind it?

"If he were dead, would it be breaking your heart, Kate?" asked MacTee.

"He's not dead, Angus," said the girl. "I know the two of you. I know that better friends never lived in the world than you are. If Danny were dead, you couldn't speak of him with a still eye, Angus."

"I was his friend," agreed Angus MacTee, with a ponderous sigh. "But now I'm thinking that it might be better for Dan if he were under the ground."

He turned away, slightly, from the girl. And Harrigan closed his hands to fists.

"What's happened to him?" asked Kate Malone.

"Whiskey got him," answered MacTee. "Whiskey got poor Dan. It was so that I didn't care to let him go to town alone. He'd spend the money I gave him for groceries, on nothing but whiskey. I'd have to go in afterwards, and I'd find him with his money spent, singing in a saloon for more drinks, or holding out his hand on a street corner . . . ."

Harrigan leaned his forehead against the trunk of a tree and fought back the growl that was rising in his throat.

"Poor Danny!" cried the girl. "I know how it is with great big impulsive natures like his. Oh, poor Danny."

Life returned to Harrigan as he listened.

"If that was only the worst." MacTee sighed. "But it's not the worst. Whiskey takes hold of a man, Kate, and rots the heart in him. Whiskey turns the soul in a man. Poor Harrigan. I'm afraid he's done for now. The law's after him, Kate."

"For what?" she cried.

"Don't talk of it, Kate," muttered MacTee. "Don't have words about it. I wouldn't breathe it even to you. Murder's not a thing to be talked about, is it?"

"Murder!" she gasped. Then: "I've got to go to him, Angus. He needs me, and I've got to go to him!"

"Eh?" grunted MacTee, staggered by this result of his talk.

"I've always sworn that, if either of you were in trouble, I'd go around the world to help you. And he needs me now."

"You'd do him good if he were like his old self," said MacTee, shaking his head. "But there's little left of the old Dan Harrigan. Ah, when I think of the eye of him, and the fire in his hair, and the fire in his heart, Kate, it's a pitiful thing to think of the man he is now, with his hair turning gray, and his eyes dim, and his face all bloated. He looks old, Kate, and weak. The soul's gone out of him. He wouldn't want to lay eyes on you, Kate. It would remind him of the man he once was, and he wouldn't want to lay eyes on you. It would remind him of the days when he was a man, and when he loved Kate Malone . . . if he really loved you,

Kate. But I've always thought it was just that he saw I wanted you, and so he wanted you, too. Except for him, tell me the truth of it, Kate . . . you and I would have been married long ago. You never would have run away from me, except for Dan Harrigan."

"I won't talk of it, Angus," said the girl. "If Danny were here, I might try. But not when he's away."

"It's Harrigan that you loved, then?" exclaimed MacTee, with a terrible scowl. "When you ran away and left word behind you, you said in the letter that you really loved one of us, but you wouldn't choose him for fear the other of us would be murdering the lucky one."

"You know well how it was," answered Kate Malone. "I owed my life to you both. You were greater friends than I've ever seen in the world. But if I married one of you, the other one would be unhappy. And men like you and Dan, Angus, are sure to use your hands, when you're unhappy. That was why I ran away. But if Danny is ill, I've got to find him. You must take me to him, Angus."

"He won't need to take you, Kate," said the great Harrigan, and stepped out from his shelter.

She put out her hands toward him. He saw the terror of inquiry turn to joy in her eyes. She ran to him and he leaned over her and kissed her.

"Angus, Angus," said the girl. "How could you have played such a joke on me, with Danny standing there all the time?"

MacTee was black, indeed. His great hands hooked themselves into predacious claws. His body trembled with passion. But he strove to cover this emotion with a harsh, grinding laugh.

"I wanted to surprise you, Kate," said MacTee. "And then have old Danny jump out like a jack-in-the-box. Good old Danny!"

Cheerfully he smote the shoulder of Harrigan, a blow that would have felled an ordinary man.

"Damn your black heart, you sneaking traitor," murmured Harrigan, adding aloud: "Well, well . . . old Angus! He carried it pretty far, though. 'Bloated face' . . . eh? There's the bright young wit for you. There's the boy to make the crowd laugh. Kate, let me look at you. Let me soak you up with my eyes. God bless me, it's a happy day, even if there's a Black MacTee in it!"

Her blue eyes were shining into the blue eyes of Harrigan. But the joy bubbling up in her grew suddenly dim, when she heard Harrigan end on the remark about MacTee.

"I wouldn't want to spoil any party," said MacTee coldly. "I'll step along, Kate. You and Dan seem to have a lot to say to each other."

"Stop it, Angus!" she exclaimed. "Stop it, Dan. You're glaring at one another like two wolves. Can't we be three friends together? Can't we . . . ?" She stopped, with a groan of despair.

"Sure," said Harrigan. "We're all friends together."

But still his eyes were fastened on those of MacTee, blue fire on black fire.

And the girl, glancing from one to the other, turned pale. The happiness was gone from her as suddenly as it had come.

But she made herself say cheerfully: "We'll take a walk together, and talk over everything since we were last together. I'll just run up to the house for ten minutes to change these shoes, and then we'll take a stroll over the hills. Wait here."

She hurried up among the trees toward the house, turning once to wave and smile toward them, before disappearing.

V

When they were alone, each of them took a long stride that left them closely confronting one another.

"Only one of us is going to be here when she comes back," said MacTee.

"Aye," answered Harrigan. "Only one of us. You murdering thug, I'm going to take everything out of you. You ran off with the mule. You left me to starve at the mine. You chucked away our money. You planted the railroad dicks along the trail to salt me down with lead if they had a chance. But all that's nothing. You had to lie to Kate Malone about me. You had to tell her that I'm a worthless drunk. Damn you, I'm going to take all of that out of you."

"I told her the truth about what you're going to be, Harrigan," said MacTee. "Because when I get through with you, today, you're going to be afraid to lift your head and look even a Chinaman in the face. I'm going to grind you so damn' small, Harrigan, that the wind can blow you away."

"Perhaps," said Harrigan, "but not just now."

"You're turning yellow already, are you?" demanded MacTee. "You're trying to back down, are you? You're a rat."

"MacTee," said Harrigan, "all the soul of me is itching in my hands. But we can't fight it out now. She'll be back before we could finish. Only, I promise you that you'll have your chance before the day's ended. We're going to take a walk, now, with Kate. We're going to be polite to each other. And tomorrow, one of us will either be dead or gone away. Is that right?"

MacTee, after fixing a glance of terrible disdain on Harrigan for a moment, turned on his heel and strode off to a small distance. He began to walk up and down, wrapped in his dark thoughts.

But Harrigan leaned against a tree and smoked a cigarette, and watched Angus MacTee. Dimly there passed through his mind the many pictures of the days when he had walked at the side of Angus MacTee into the face of dangers that they had met together. They had wrought such deeds for one another that the whole wide West had spoken of them. They had been such friends as men conceive, but never find.

Of these things, however, Harrigan saw only the faint pictures. For now they wanted one woman. In the old days they had done battle for her. Matched in strength, in craft, in desperate courage, Red Dan Harrigan and Black Angus MacTee had struggled to win her, until in the end she had fled from them both for fear that they would kill one another. She had told them that they would never see her again. She had told them, in her last letter, that she truly loved one of them. But her choice she would not name.

When she was gone, they were to each other more than brothers. But now that she was with them again, they mutually poisoned the air for one another.

All this was the mind of Harrigan, as he stared at MacTee. When they were together at the mine, the vigilance of MacTee in acts of courtesy and in kindness never ended. He was always first to find the water jar empty and to assume the labor of filling it. He was the first to forage for wood. He labored willingly extra hours sharpening the drills. The money in his pocket was Harrigan's money; the blood in his body was Harrigan's blood; the breath of his nostrils he would give up for his friend. But not Kate Malone!

When she entered their world, MacTee became a dark and crafty savage. A wild Indian was capable of no more atrocities. His fruitful malevolence had scattered a hundred dangers along the trail that Harrigan had just followed. It would scatter more, in the future. So there arose in Harrigan a red flame of detestation and hatred. If Kate Malone were removed, he knew that he and MacTee were welded as one flesh and one blood and one bone. That was the very reason she had fled from them before.

Suddenly Harrigan said: "MacTee, it's more than ten minutes we've been waiting."

"Ah?" muttered MacTee.

"It's nearer to fifteen," said Harrigan.

"What would you mean by that, and glaring at me?" asked MacTee.

"I'd mean," said Harrigan, "that you let the brute beast come out in your face, a minute ago, and she could see it plain enough. She's gone again . . . I'll bet my soul on it. She's gone again."

MacTee gave him one stern glance. "Maybe you're right. But it's the red hell that shone out of you that she saw."

They were already dashing through the woods toward the house.

"I might have guessed . . ." groaned Harrigan.

He strained with all his might to gain the lead. It seemed to him that in this contest the supremacy between them would be established. But when they issued from the trees before the house, MacTee was a stride in the lead.

Instantly they saw the answer to their fears. On a distant hill a rider wavered for an instant on the horizon, then disappeared from their view. It was a woman. It must be Kate Malone.

"Damn you!" hissed Harrigan, and smote the dark granite of the jaw of MacTee.

Stone is hard, but iron is harder, and the fist of Harrigan was iron. MacTee was hurled to the ground, and Harrigan ran toward a big, brown gelding that was tethered in front of the ranch house.

"Hey, boss you ain't runnin' off with that hoss, are you?" shouted the cook.

Harrigan answered merely: "I'll send back the price in hard cash."

He untethered the rope with flying fingers. He had his foot in the stirrup, when a thunderbolt struck him to the ground. It was Angus MacTee.

And it was Angus MacTee who leaped into the saddle. Harrigan rose and laid his mighty clutch on the reins, reaching for the gun hand of MacTee at the same time, and locking his hold on the wrist.

Then a calm voice said behind them: "You two hoss thieves, get away from that mustang."

They looked toward the house and saw on the verandah a little man with a long rifle leveled firmly at his shoulder.

There is no arguing with a rifle held by such hands. One may gamble against a revolver, but not against a rifleman who kills his deer at six hundred yards.

So MacTee dismounted and stood at the side of Harrigan.

"I oughta hold you and jail you, maybe," said the rancher. "But all I'll do is to get you off my place. Move, the pair of you." He raised his voice to an angry yell, as he lost control of his temper. "Get!" he cried.

MacTee and Harrigan got.

They strode rapidly across the rolling ground until they found the trail of the horse that had carried the girl away from them. They came to the hilltop over which she had dropped from view. There they paused.

They glared at one another with gloomy detestation. On the jaw of MacTee there was a red lump. On the side of Harrigan's face was its mate.

"Harrigan," said MacTee. "I'm going to break you open like a crab and eat the heart out of you, before long."

"MacTee," said Harrigan, "there's nothing here but the sky and the grass to look at us. I'm better than you with a gun. I'll put it aside. I'll have you with my bare hands. There'll be more taste to the killing of you, that way."

"Harrigan," said MacTee, "it's a true thing that I'd love to be at you. But we've got a job on our hands that may use up the brains of both of us. Look yonder!"

He pointed toward the wide landscape, the green hills, and the ragged storm of mountains that rose toward the horizon.

"There's our job. Kate's no fool. She's as tough as whipcord, and she'll run like a fox till she thinks that she's dropped us off her trail. She's dropped us before. She'll drop us again, unless we put our heads together and all the strength that's in us. Let's be partners again till we've found her. And afterwards . . . God help you, Harrigan."

Red Dan Harrigan grinned. He held out his hand.

"I'll be a brother to you, MacTee," he said, "till we've found her. And after that, MacTee, I'll work you into a red mud, with my hands."

Their hands closed, joining with a mighty pressure.

VI

They traveled through the rest of that day as only Harrigan and MacTee could travel. If there was more speed in MacTee's long legs over the level, there was more agility in Harrigan when they came to rough country. In the evening, they came to a little ranch house on the southern side of a hill. In a big field near the house and barn, horses were grazing.

Said MacTee: "We've got to have horses, if we want to find Kate Malone."

"We've got to find horses," agreed Harrigan. "But you know this part of the world, MacTee. They'd rather hang a horse thief than a murderer, Angus."

"There was never a rope spun that could hang me," said Angus MacTee. "If there's no heart in you, Harrigan, turn back, now, and I'll go on alone."

"How could a Scotchman have the heart of a Harrigan?" asked the other. "I'll go wherever you'll go, MacTee, and do whatever you'll do, and then one step beyond."

"Go into that barn, then, and find saddles and bridles," said MacTee calmly, "and ropes. When you've got 'em, I'll catch the horses. I'm not as good a thief as you are. There's not much cat in me. But I can handle a rope."

It might seem an unfair division of the labor for Harrigan to risk the danger of men, and MacTee to take only the task of catching up horses. But Red Harrigan was not one to split straws. He circled the hill on which the ranch buildings stood, came over the shoulder of it, and passed out of the twilight into the thick, muddy black of the interior of the barn. Suddenly out of the darkness he heard the overbearing powerful neigh of a stallion. A horse began to plunge and batter inside a box stall. Harrigan groaned, for the people in the ranch house were sure to hear this uproar and respond to it. He was not surprised when, far away, he heard a screen door slam with a tin-pan jingling.

He had found saddles and saddle blankets and bridles. And now hurried back with them toward the rear door. He was not yet at it when the other door opened.

Harrigan, leaping eagerly into the outer night, found that he was lighted by the brightening moonlight. A man shouted loudly: "Stop, thief!"

Harrigan kicked the door shut behind him and ran into the field, the corner where MacTee was already holding a pair of mustangs. He reached MacTee, who held the horses steady while Harrigan began the saddling in frantic haste.

The near door of the barn opened. Harrigan groaned. But he could hear the man who stood in the entrance swearing angrily, apparently unable to see anything suspicious.

The rancher fired twice, but the bullets came nowhere near the two thieves. Then he cried out, loudly, as other men came running from the house.

But Harrigan and MacTee were already spurring away. The instant they were seen, bullets came whirring. But what can a revolver do at long range when it is fired by moonlight? They rode straight on up a narrow valley, the floor of which grew steeper and steeper.

MacTee began to laugh. "Dan, d'ye hear me? Isn't it like the old days? Were there ever any better days than the old ones?"

And Dan Harrigan laughed, too. He forgot Kate Malone. He forgot the very object of his quest. It seemed to him that there was nothing in the world that was half so important as the great Black MacTee, the companion who never failed a man in time of danger.

Behind them came the noise of hoofs. But the two merely laughed again, in the highest indifference. Mere mortals could not be matched against a Red Harrigan and a Black MacTee.

For two hours, off and on, they heard the distant noise of the pursuit. Twice rifles were fired after them. Then they were left alone to travel deeper into the night.

"Suppose that she left this trail?" asked Harrigan.

"She'd keep to the valley," answered MacTee. "I know the way her mind works. She'd keep to this valley. She'd want to get those mountains for a fence between her and Harrigan and MacTee."

A wind struck them, iced by the high mountain snows. But they held steadily on, crossed the divide, and came down through tall forests. At last, staring through a gap in the woods, they made out the wide-spread, gleaming lights of a town.

"That's where she is," said MacTee with great assurance. "There's no use killing the horses. We'll go down in the morning, and find her there."

"She'll start on before the morning," said Harrigan.

"She can't keep running all the way around the world," answered MacTee. "No, she'll stay there for a while and hope that we'll never find her. We'd better camp here."

So they camped. They built a bed of evergreen boughs and were soon asleep. And when they wakened, the sky was luminous with the dawn. They resaddled the horses, pulled up their belts a notch, and jogged the mustangs down toward the town.

It was sprawled like a spider, with a small body and with long arms that stretched up many narrow gulches roundabout. Twenty trails converged on that small city.

"It's a jumping-off place," said Harrigan gloomily. "She might have gone in any direction."

"We'll find her," said MacTee. "There's something in me that knows how to find her as sure as a magnet knows how to find north."

The trail down was slow work. It was very rough and entailed constant windings that absorbed much time. The sun was high and hot when at last they dropped into the hollow where the town lay.

MacTee wanted to go straight to the hotel.

"Suppose a pair of stolen horses have been trailed as far as this town?" suggested Harrigan uneasily.

"We have to take chances," answered MacTee. "And in the hotel, we'll find people who'll know every stray dog that's entered the town in the last ten years."

They reached the hotel, which was a square white box shouldered tightly in between adjoining buildings, with the usual verandah strung across the face of it. In a livery stable across the street they put up the horses, then entered the hotel. They washed and shaved, and went into the dining room.

It was after 8 a.m., and, therefore, very late for breakfast in a Western town. The chairs were standing on tables. A big fellow with a tattooed arm of a sailor was scrubbing the floor with a pail of suds and a stable broom.

"Too late, brother," he growled over his shoulder at the pair.

MacTee took two chairs from a small table and put them in place.

"Ham and eggs, coffee, hot cakes, and anything else that's handy," he said.

The waiter walked up to him with a scowl.

"Are you tryin' to start something?" he demanded.

MacTee put the end of a forefinger against the breast of the ex-sailor. It was like touching him with a rod of steel.

"What I start, I finish," said MacTee. "Unless you want to be close to the end, move some chuck out of the kitchen and into this room. Understand?"

The waiter understood. He moved his glance in a small arc, from the third button of MacTee's shirt to his gleaming eyes.

"All right," said the waiter, and nodded.

MacTee and Harrigan sat down. "Danny," said MacTee, "I wish that we'd never laid eyes on Kate Malone."

"I wish it, too," said Harrigan, "except when I think of her."

"She's nothing," said MacTee, "but a snip of a girl with a brown face and blue eyes. There's a thousand prettier than she is. What is she to come between friends like you and me?"

Harrigan frowned and shook his head.

"I'd like to agree with you, Angus," he said. "But I'm just after seeing her. Besides, you'd never hold to the idea that you have right now. Not if you thought that I had Kate Malone."

"No," agreed MacTee suddenly. He jarred the heavy table with one fist. "You and I have fought for her and starved for her and bled for her too many times. I couldn't give her up to you, Danny. But I could wish that another man would come and take her. Not like you. Not my kind of a man. But some damned long-haired violin player that I couldn't touch for the fear of mashing him like a rotten apple. If a sneaking fool like that should come along and walk off with Kate Malone, Harrigan, I'd be a happy man, after a while. After the poison boiled down in me, I'd be a happy man."

The waiter came in, but not with a stack of dishes piled on his arm. Instead, he came with an armed man walking on each side of him, and behind this leading trio there moved others, a whole dozen or more of stalwarts.

Harrigan gave them one side glance. "They've come for us, Angus," he said.

"There's hardly a round dozen of 'em," answered MacTee calmly. "And if they knew us, Danny . . . if they knew us as we know ourselves . . . wouldn't the fools bring the whole town together before they tried to come at the bare hands of Harrigan and MacTee?"

He who walked on the right hand of the waiter was built like a lumberjack and dressed like a lumberjack in a plain Mackinaw. On the lapel of the coat was a steel badge, brighter than silver.

He was such a big man that he did not touch a weapon, in making this arrest. He merely stepped to the table and rapped his brown knuckles on the top of it.

"Stand up, you bohunks," he said. "Hoss thieves get free board and room, in this here town of Yellow Gulch."

VII

Harrigan looked at the deputy sheriff and at the fellows ranging beside him, and realized that they were men.

"All right," he said to MacTee, "I guess we'll have to stick up our hands, partner."

"We will," said MacTee, and, rising to his feet, he brought up his fist like the head of an iron mace. It bashed the deputy sheriff under the jaw and sent him staggering across the floor. Harrigan selected the ex-sailor who had betrayed them. It was neither an uppercut nor a swing or a straight punch that he used, but his favorite hook. The hook of Harrigan was like the snapping of a whiplash, with an anvil hitched to the end of the lash. His blow struck the jaw of the waiter, and that unfortunate man fell on his hands and knees.

Then Harrigan and MacTee raised a frightful yell and charged home among the men of Yellow Gulch. Whoever they struck fell or staggered far away. That single charge should have ended the fight at once, for guns could not be used in the tangled heart of this mêlée.

But Harrigan saw a strange thing. The men of Yellow Gulch might be felled, but they would not stay down. The deputy sheriff, the first to drop, was already on his feet and coming straight into the thick of the fight. The ex-sailor was up, also, and charging. And all the other men of Yellow Gulch came in with cheerful shouts. Their eyes shone, and it was plain that they considered this a delightful game. Their bodies were of India rubber—their jaws were of whalebone—and their souls were the purest flame of battle.

Just as Harrigan finished these observations, two ponderous fists landed on his jaw from opposite sides. He dropped on his face.

When he wakened, a pair of monstrous legs bestrode him. It was MacTee, bellowing like a mad bull, striking right and left.

As Harrigan gathered his feet and hands under the weight of his body, the men of Yellow Gulch fell back a little, and the deputy sheriff stood before MacTee with a gun in either hand.

The deputy sheriff was no longer what he had been. The left side of his face was a great red puff. His right eye was closed. His coat was half ripped from his body.

"Stick up those hands, or I'll blow you to hell!" shouted the deputy sheriff.

But Harrigan dived along the floor, struck the legs from beneath the man of the law, and, as the revolvers drilled eyeholes for the sunlight through the wall, Harrigan arose again into the fight.

"Harrigan!" thundered MacTee, a drunken joy in his voice, as he saw that his friend was again in the fight. "Harrigan!" he roared as though it were a battle cry.

He caught up a chair and swung it.

"Harrigan!" he bellowed. "Harrigan!"

With each shout, he struck down a man. Half the little crowd of Yellow Gulch warriors was on the floor, and through the rest Harrigan and MacTee charged to the side entrance to the dining room.

They heard an uproar of pursuit behind them. As Harrigan slammed and locked the door behind them, a bullet clipped through and split one panel. But the door held, nevertheless, while the two fugitives sprinted with lengthened legs down a narrow alley, and straight out of the little town of Yellow Gulch into the woods.

* * * * *

The green of the trees covered them. And presently they were sitting at the side of a little brook that wandered through the forest.

They smoked cigarettes, considered the brightness of the patches of the sun, and the brown of shadows upon pine needles, and listened to the quiet conversation of the flowing water.

Finally MacTee announced: "We were licked and chucked out. We were chucked out with no breakfast, even. What's the matter with us, Harrigan? We used to rate as men. Now what are we?"

Harrigan shook his head. He was peeling off his clothes, and, when he had finished that task, he stepped into the water of the brook and scrubbed from himself the signs of battle. At last he redressed and lay on the bank in the shadow.

"This Yellow Gulch," he observed, at the last, "is the sort of a town that we ought to know a whole lot more about, MacTee. It's full of folks that I could be glad to see, and so could you."

"I could," agreed MacTee. "It's a town worth having and a town worth knowing. Did you see that yellow-headed fellow with the straight left?"

"I did," said Harrigan, caressing his face. "And there was the short man with the big shoulders and the over-arm swing. You remember him?"

"*Ugh!*" grunted MacTee. "I couldn't plant him with a solid sock. Did you cop him?"

"I just managed to hit him in the pit of the belly, and, as he dropped, I was able to uppercut him, and, when he straightened from that, I clouted him on the jaw."

"With a hook?" asked MacTee.

"With a hook," said Harrigan.

"Danny," said MacTee dreamily, "there's times when I love you more than a brother. What did he look like when you last saw him? I sort of missed him in the last few minutes."

"He looked like an astronomer," said Harrigan, after a moment of thought. "He was lying on his back and he seemed to be studying the stars."

MacTee laughed broodingly.

Harrigan said: "Are we beaten, MacTee, or what do you say?"

"The mountains are up and against us," said MacTee.

"They are," agreed Harrigan. "But if we lose her now, we'll never find her."

"Now," said MacTee, "that they know the quality of us, they'll be shooting on sight. And these people, they wouldn't know how to miss."

"They would not," agreed Harrigan.

"So what do you suggest?" asked MacTee.

"I suggest," said Harrigan, "that we draw straws to see who goes into Yellow Gulch after dark and tries his best to get on the track of her."

MacTee shuddered. "Draw to see who goes back into Yellow Gulch?" he echoed.

"That's the idea," said Harrigan.

MacTee groaned. "All right," he said. "Pick out some straws, and we'll see."

Harrigan picked two blades of grass. The short one he laid under his thumb projecting less than the long one. Then he changed his mind and laid them with their ends exactly even.

"The long man goes to Yellow Gulch," said Harrigan.

"Good," said MacTee, and straightway picked the shorter of the pair.

Harrigan stared, opening his palm to reveal the long one.

"Well," said Harrigan, "that's the way I'd rather have it."

"You're a brave man, Danny," said MacTee. "And when we're this far from Kate, I don't mind saying that you're as brave as any man in the world. But you wouldn't be telling me that you'd rather be going into Yellow Gulch than sitting out here in the woods, waiting for news?"

"I would, though," argued Harrigan. "If I sat here, and you went in, I'd go mad. For I'd see you finding Kate Malone, for yourself. And I'd see you talking to her, persuading and lying, until you got her for yourself."

"She's not there at all, most likely," said MacTee.

"Maybe not," said Harrigan. "But I'll go fishing in Yellow Gulch for her as soon as it's dark . . . and I'll be a happy man to start on my way."

VIII

MacTee went to the edge of the woods with Harrigan, where he looked with his friend at the glitter of the town lights.

"You're a brave man, Harrigan," he said, "considering the sort of men they have in Yellow Gulch. Good bye, and God bless you. If a thing happens wrong to you, I'll find the man that did it, and plant him alive."

So Harrigan went like a thief into the town.

If MacTee dreaded the place and the strong-handed men of it, so did Harrigan. But in his heart there was the wild and eerie passion that led him toward the girl.

So he went on until, upon the dark of an alley, a kitchen door opened, a dull shaft of yellow lamplight fell upon Harrigan, and a woman's voice shouted: "It's Harrigan! It's Harrigan!"

Harrigan ran.

It was as though the woman had called to furious hornets, all in readiness inside of a nest. Out they poured, the men of Yellow Gulch, to follow him. Doors slammed. The heavy feet of men hit the ground.

He fled across the main street, a gorge of revealing light that brought a shower of bullets after him. One of them kissed the tip of his right ear.

He bounded like a deer into a silent byway. A tall board fence rose beside it. He leaped, caught the top rim, swung himself over, and started for the fence on the opposite side.

Then the imp of the perverse made him decide to trust to his luck—so he dropped into a nest of high grass and lay still. At the same time, a pursuer swung over the top of the fence like a pole-vaulter, and another and another followed him.

180

What manner of men were these in Yellow Gulch, when all of them seemed able to match the best that Harrigan could do? His heart grew small in him, with wonder, and he shook his head as he lay in the tall grass, murmuring: "I must be pretty far West."

A dozen, he counted, crossed the yard, vaulted the fence on the farther side, and rushed away. Other footfalls stormed through the street. Then gunshots broke out, far away. The noise diminished, the shouting turned corners and was obscured.

After that, a quiet footfall drew near to Harrigan. Then the voice of a girl said: "I've got a sawed-off shotgun loaded with buckshot. I've got you covered, and I can't miss. Get up out of that, Harrigan."

Harrigan got up, at once. With a sawed-off shotgun, no matter in what hands, argument is futile. He saw that the girl was small. He saw that the gun in her hands was real. So he lifted his arms above his head. This was something for the world to read in newspapers and laugh at—how Harrigan was captured by a girl, by a child.

"March up there through that screen door into the kitchen," said the girl. "And if you try to jump one side or the other, I'll blow you out of your socks."

If they had men in Yellow Gulch, they had women, also. Harrigan walked a chalk line to the back verandah, up the steps, and through the screen door of the kitchen. He faced the stove, his arms still lifted over his head. The screen door creaked gently behind him.

"All right," said the girl. "You can turn around."

He turned. She was not more than sixteen. She had freckles across her nose. She was rather small. But her eyes were of the divine Irish blue.

"So you're Harrigan," she said.

"I'm a piece of him," said Harrigan.

"It's you that licked Jim Bingham, is it?" said the girl.

"Who's Jim Bingham?"

"You licked him, and you don't even know his name? He's my brother."

"I know him, then," said Harrigan. "He's short and wide and he knows how to box. He's got black hair and a pair of eyes in his head."

"I'm mighty glad you noticed him," said the girl.

"Molly!" groaned a voice at a distance of two or three rooms.

"Aye, Jim. Wait a minute." She added: "He's lying in there with a couple of busted ribs. But you don't look so big. Not to me, you don't."

"I'm not so big," said Harrigan gently.

"But you licked Jim," she said grimly, bitterly.

"I had the weight and the reach on him," said Harrigan.

"You had ten or twelve Huskies socking at you, too," she answered, shaking her head. "I thought the Binghams were the best, but I guess they're not. The Harrigans must be close to the top."

"I got in a lucky punch," said Harrigan.

"Harrigan," said the girl, "why do you and MacTee steal horses and chase around after a girl that doesn't want you?"

"Who says that?"

"There's talk around."

"The talk's wrong," said Harrigan. "She wants one of us. We want to find which one."

"Ah?" said the girl.

"Yes. She wants one of us."

"She's mighty pretty," said the girl. "I saw her. She's beautiful. She's good, too, and she's kind, and gentle, and wise, and brave, and everything."

"Yes. She's everything," agreed Harrigan. "I've known her for a long time. I've known her since she was a ringer for you."

"Since she was what? Are you trying to flatter me, Harrigan?"

"The truth is not flattering," answered Harrigan. "I remember her when she was a ringer for you. And I've been following her ever since."

"Never mind who she's a ringer for," said Molly Bingham, flushing. "But go on and tell me what makes you think she wants one of you?"

"She said so, one day."

"It was a long time ago, then," suggested the girl.

"Yes, it was a long time ago," agreed Harrigan, sighing.

"Suppose that she took MacTee," said the girl. "What would you do?"

"I'd murder the black Scotch heart of him," said Harrigan.

The girl started. "I think you mean it," she answered. "And yet you and MacTee fight for each other like two brothers."

"He's the best man in the world," agreed Harrigan, "except where Kate Malone's concerned."

At this, the girl chuckled softly.

"Molly!" called her brother, in angry impatience.

"Be still, Jimmy. I'm coming in a moment," answered the girl.

"How did you know me?" asked Harrigan.

"I saw the red of your hair," answered the girl. "And who else but a Harrigan or a MacTee would be leaping the fences around Yellow Gulch at this time of the night?"

"True," said Harrigan. "I hadn't thought about that."

"I'm going to call for help," said Molly Bingham.

"If you do," answered Harrigan, "they'll never take me alive."

"Well, then," she replied, "I'll give you a chance. I'll send you to where Kate Malone is staying. But I'll have a promise out of you, first."

"I'll promise you the clouds out of the sky," said Harrigan.

"Harrigan," said the girl, "she loves either you or MacTee, and neither of you can guess which one it is. And she doesn't dare to give herself to one of you for fear that the other will make mincemeat of the lucky man. But now I'm going to take your word of honor that you'll go to her, Harrigan, and swear on the Bible to her that, if she loves MacTee, you'll do him no harm, but you'll go far away. Will you promise me that?"

Harrigan looked up at the ceiling, then down into the face of the girl. "Well . . ." he said.

"Or else I'll raise a yell that'll bring all of the town to this spot. It's a mean town, too, Harrigan. There's a dozen of its best men that are wearing bumps and breaks because of you and MacTee, and all their friends, and themselves, are achin' to have another go at you."

"It's true," said Harrigan. "It's a tough town. The toughest that ever I found in my days."

"Will you promise me?"

"If she says that it's MacTee, will I go way off and never do him a harm?" repeated Harrigan.

"Aye. Will you promise that?"

"Yes," groaned the hesitant Harrigan.

"Good," said the girl. "Give your hand on it."

She held out hers.

Harrigan looked at the hand and sighed.

"Be a man, Harrigan," said the girl.

Gingerly he took her hand. He closed his eyes, and sighed.

"Here's my promise," said Harrigan, "and God help me. Where'll I find her?"

"I know where she is," said Molly Bingham. "Go out to the front corner of the garden. Wait there. I'll soon be coming."

Harrigan went out through the darkness of a trance and stood in the garden. Presently the front door opened and closed. The girl stood beside him.

"Come with me," she said.

Harrigan followed her down a lane, and across an alley, and up a barren, empty street until they came to a little house retired among trees.

"She's in there," said the girl. "Wouldn't you feel shame, Dan Harrigan, to be hounding a girl like her, and making the world talk? Wouldn't you feel shame?"

But she was laughing softly, as she walked up the path before him to the house.

When they came to the trees, she said: "Wait here."

He waited. She went on. She climbed the steps through a soft shaft of lamplight. She knocked at the front door, then opened it and went inside.

Harrigan heard nothing. The coldness of ice water welled up in him, covered his heart, rose as high as his throat. He felt dizzy, and weak.

At last the front door of the house opened. Two women came out. One of them sat down at the top of the steps, and he knew that this was Molly Bingham.

The other came with hesitant steps down the path. At last she reached a full halt, turned, and beckoned. Molly Bingham instantly ran and joined her. They came on together. A dullness of lamplight passed over them, and Harrigan saw the face of Kate Malone. His dizziness increased. He wanted to run away, leaving all questions unasked and unanswered.

Then they were close. Kate Malone halted.

The younger girl stamped on the gravel of the path. "Come on to her, then, you great hulk," she said.

Harrigan strode looming through the darkness. When he came to Kate Malone, he dropped to one knee, and felt that it was the weakness of his legs that compelled him.

She made a gesture toward him. He caught her hand. It was cold and trembling.

"Poor Danny," she said. "Did the brutes hurt you badly?"

At that, a wild hope filled him.

"Fists couldn't be hurting me, Kate!" he exclaimed. "Nothing but a word from you could hurt me. That's what I've come to learn from you. Tell me, Kate, that you love MacTee, and I'll take myself from your way. I'll never bother Angus. You'll be free with him, and God give you both happiness. But tell me the truth of it. Do you love Angus MacTee?"

He listened breathlessly. The pause was long. The moments of it stung him like poisoned daggers.

Then she answered in a broken voice: "Aye, Danny . . . I love him."

IX

The hope sickened and died in Harrigan as a green twig withers and droops in flame. After a while, he got up to his feet. He kept on rising when he was erect. He kept on drawing himself straighter and straighter, drawing in deeper breaths, telling himself silently that he would not die, that men did not die of wounds that words could make.

Someone was weeping. Well, that was like Kate Malone. She could not endure giving pain, and she was an old friend and a dear one. Yes, Kate would weep over him. This made tears sting his own eyes, until suddenly he saw that it was the other girl who was crying heartily, stifling her sobs.

But Kate stood with her hands clasped in front of her, and her face lifted toward the stars. She reminded him of a picture he had seen somewhere, he could not remember where.

He said: "Well, Kate, I'm taking myself away. If I were man enough, I'd go out into the woods and tell Angus that he's the lucky one. But I couldn't trust myself that far. If I looked at the face of Black Angus, and thought of him calling you his wife . . . I'd likely go mad. But I've sworn an oath and given my hand on it . . . and now take your word and leave you."

He held out his hand. The cold hand of Kate was laid in his.

"You blithering idiot!" gasped Molly Bingham. "I never knew a red-headed man to be such a fool. Kiss her good bye . . . and then see."

There was a melancholy stirring in the soul of Harrigan.

"We've been through great things, Kate," he said. "Will you kiss me good bye?"

He put his left arm around her, gently.

She had not stirred, but still looked past him at the upper night. She was like a stone.

"Oh, Dan Harrigan, you half-wit," said Molly Bingham. "You swore that you'd leave her if she loved MacTee. But make her swear your own oath that she loves him. Make her swear that it's true she loves MacTee."

"Almighty thunder!" groaned Harrigan.

His left arm was no longer gentle. It crushed Kate Malone to him.

"Swear it, by God, Kate, and I'll leave you. Swear that you love MacTee. For if you don't mean it with all your heart . . . if it's only a trick to get me and all the murdering trouble out of the way . . . . Swear that you love him, Kate. The saying of it won't do with me."

But Kate Malone began to sob.

And that baffled Harrigan. It made him more bewildered than ever.

"She's only a poor liar, after all," said Molly Bingham. "Kiss her, Dan Harrigan, and see what's left of her pretending. Kiss her . . . the silly baby."

But Molly Bingham was herself crying, and talking through her tears. And Harrigan knew that in all the days of his life he never would understand women truly.

He leaned to touch his lips to the face of Kate Malone. Her head dropped weakly against the hollow of his shoulder.

"Kate!" he cried out in an ecstasy of revelation. "You're mine. You belong to me! It isn't MacTee that you care for."

"It's you, Danny," said the girl. "It's always been you. But I've never dared to show what I feel, for fear of Angus MacTee. What can we do now? He'll kill you, Dan, if he finds out the truth."

"God means it to come to a showdown between us," said Harrigan. "I've got to see MacTee, and face him . . . and have it out."

"No!" cried the girl. "You'd never come back to me alive!"

"I've got to tell him that I've found you," said Harrigan. "I came in for both of us to find your trail, Kate. We're partners, Angus and I. We'll keep on being partners . . . till he goes for my throat. There's no other honest way out of it."

"Would you be honest with the devil, Dan Harrigan?" asked Molly hotly. "Well, no matter what MacTee would do to a man, he'll never touch a girl. Let me know where to find him, and I'll take him the word that you've found Kate, and that you and she are away together. I don't have to tell what the direction is."

"I can't let you go out and face him," said Harrigan.

"It's the one way to live up to your partnership with him," said Molly briskly. "If you talk to him, you know it'll be the death of both of you. Tell me where to find him."

"Tell her," said Kate Malone.

So Harrigan hesitantly, uncertainly gave the word to Molly of how she could pass through the woods and come to the creek, and so to the camp of Black MacTee.

"I'll be on my way," said Molly. "Kate, do up your things. Get out of Yellow Gulch with Harrigan. Take the Dormer Pass and head straight for the railroad. You'll be out of the reach of MacTee before long. Go fast! You have your own horse, Kate. And in the shed behind my house there's a big bay gelding that belongs to nobody but me. You can take that horse, Dan Harrigan. Good bye, Kate! Good bye, Harrigan!"

"Wait!" exclaimed Kate Malone. "Stop her, Danny!"

Harrigan barred the way of Molly. At the touch of his hand, she was still, laughing and trembling with excitement.

"What am I to say to you, Molly, darling?" said Kate. "And what's Dan to say to you? We'll owe you everything."

"I could teach Dan what to say to me," said Molly. "If I were a year or two older, I'd fight you for him, Kate. Dan, if you lose her somewhere in the mountains, come back and you can find me."

She slipped away and was instantly lost in the darkness. She had given them the means of escaping, and now she was determined to assure their safety still further, so that no harm whatever could overtake them . . . .

Running as fast as any boy, she got to the house of the deputy sheriff. He sat on his front porch with a wet towel around his head and various swellings discoloring his face.

"Hello, Dave," said the girl. "I've got news for you that'll make you open both eyes."

"It'll be a month before I get both eyes wide open," said the deputy sheriff. He had the shamelessness of a man whose courage has been proved over and over. He sat up and took the towel from his face. "It's not mumps that I caught, but the Harrigan," he explained with a grin. "What's the good news, Molly?"

"Harrigan's gone," said the girl.

"The devil he has. Where?"

"Through the Dormer Pass with Kate Malone, and if you lift a hand to follow 'em, Dave, you're not a right man."

"Listen to her," said Dave's wife, chuckling. "I suppose she loves the red man."

"I do," said Molly. "Who wouldn't love a man that can beat Dave, here? And my own brother laid up with some broken ribs from the same fist. Of course, I love Red Harrigan. But there's a thing for you to do still. You can catch Black MacTee."

"Aye," said the deputy sheriff. "He has a fist like an iron club. I'd like to put hands on MacTee, and irons on him, too."

"You'd better have the irons on him before you try your hands," said Molly. "Get some of your best men, Dave. There are plenty in Yellow Gulch that'd be glad to be in at the killing of MacTee or of Harrigan. You know that."

"I know that," agreed Dave, "and I'll do it." He stood up from his chair. "You'll be running the whole county before long, Molly," he said. "You're running Yellow Gulch already."

"As soon as I outgrow freckles," said Molly, "I'm going to run for governor. You won't take after Harrigan, Dave?"

"No," said the deputy sheriff. "Not if you tell me to keep my hands off him. I wouldn't dare." He chuckled again. "But this MacTee. Where is he, Molly?"

"You cut across town till you come through the woods to the creek. Go up the creek till you find a sandbar with the creek spilling over the two ends of it. Black MacTee will be somewhere there. And go carefully, Dave. He's a tiger."

"I'll have five men with me," said the deputy sheriff cheerfully. "I'd rather walk into the cave of a mother grizzly than into a place where that black Scotchman is hiding."

X

Black MacTee, sitting on a rock at the side of the water, trailed his left hand in the icy current. His heart was aching with desire for a smoke, but he dared not smoke for fear that even the easily dissipated smoke of a cigarette might reach inquisitive nostrils and bring danger.

So, as he sat there, he occupied his mind and quelled his nerves by submitting his flesh to the biting chill of the stream. He was so engaged when he heard a faint rustling sound. It was a very small sound. It might have been the rustling of leaves when branches toss slightly. It might have been the step of a wild beast inside the wood.

But the nerves of MacTee were drawn taut, and therefore he lifted his head to listen. What he heard next was hardly a sound at all. It was rather a vibration, a nothingness of tremor that ran through the ground. But it sent MacTee into cover with the speed of a slinking cat. He crouched in the shadow, looking out savagely, tensely around him.

After a time, he heard another mere whisper. It was close beside him, and now he could make out the silhouette of a man moving from behind the trunk of a tree, coming toward the sandbar.

MacTee reached out his arm, massive and rigid as the walking beam of a great engine. With the sharp, deadly knuckles of his second joints, he struck the stalking silhouette behind the ear. The sound was very muffled. It was not as loud as the noise a chopper makes when it is struck into soft meat. And yet the hunting figure relaxed, at once.

MacTee, taking a single long stride forward, caught the slumping body before it could crash to the ground. With that burden in his arms, he straightened, and stalked away soundlessly.

On his left, he made out another dim form, slipping in the opposite direction, and he felt that he had been betrayed, and by Harrigan. The thought stopped his heart with cold sickness. There was no rage in him, at the moment. There was only that unutterable smallness of soul and despair as he thought that Red Dan Harrigan might have betrayed a partner.

He locked that misery behind his teeth and went on, stepping softly. When the burden he carried began to moan faintly and to stir in his arms, he was at a considerable distance from his starting point. So he put the man on his feet and shook him. Searching through his clothes, MacTee found a revolver and took it away from his captive.

"Who are you?" asked MacTee.

The other muttered: "Lord God, my head's smashed in."

"It'll feel better, after a while," said MacTee. "What d'ye mean by sneaking through the night like a mountain lion hunting mutton? Who are you?"

"I'm Deputy Sheriff Dave . . . ."

"Ah," said MacTee. "You're the deputy sheriff, eh?"

"I'm the deputy sheriff, and . . . ."

"Somebody told you that you'd find me here?"

"Yes," admitted the man of the law, his wits still reeling from the blow that he had received.

"He told you, then," muttered MacTee.

He drew in a long, long breath to keep away the sense of strangulation.

"Even Harrigan," said MacTee miserably. "Anybody else . . . but not Harrigan a traitor. Traitors don't wear red hair." He added loudly: "Where's Harrigan?"

"I don't know," said the deputy sheriff. "It's MacTee that has me? What happened?"

"What's happened doesn't matter, compared with what's going to happen pretty soon," said MacTee, "unless you tell me what's become of Harrigan. Have you caught him?"

"No."

"He's not in jail?"

"No, he's not in jail."

"Then where is he? D'you think I'll hesitate to squash your windpipe for you, unless you talk out to me, man?"

A shudder passed through the deputy sheriff. It was a tremor imparted to his body by the quivering of the angry hand of MacTee as it grasped the shoulder of the prisoner.

Far ahead of them a voice called anxiously: "Dave! Hey, Dave!"

"My God, I've made a fool of myself," groaned Dave.

"It's better to be a living fool than a dead one," said MacTee. "Tell me where Harrigan is, or . . . ."

"He's in the Dormer Pass, I suppose, by this time."

"Ha? You know where he is? In the Dormer Pass?"

"Yes. They've gotten up into it by this time."

"They? Who's with him?"

"Kate Malone," said the deputy sheriff.

"God in heaven!" groaned MacTee. "The coward, the cur, the traitor. He stole her and he's running with her?"

"She's gone willingly with him, MacTee," said the deputy sheriff. "She has . . . ."

"You lie," said MacTee, and struck him heavily in the face, so that the head of the deputy bobbed back on his shoulders.

"Where's the Dormer Pass?" asked MacTee.

"There," said the frightened deputy, for he felt that he was in the hands of a madman. "There, to the right of that sugarloaf, in that cut, yonder. That's the Dormer. You can see the cloud rolling down through it."

MacTee looked, and he saw a white serpent of mist, brightened by the moon, crawling down the face of a mountain.

"The Judas!" groaned MacTee. "The damned, sneaking, Irish blarney, hypocrite, and traitor. He stole Kate and he sent the law after Angus MacTee to keep me from . . . ."

"No," said the deputy Sheriff. "He didn't send . . . ."

"Be still, damn you!" snarled MacTee. He dashed his fist into the battered face of Dave again, with such force that the deputy slumped senselessly to the ground.

MacTee let him drop. Well ahead of him, through the trees, he could hear the shouting of several voices that blended and blurred together, and yet he could make out among them the calling of the name: "Dave!"

But there was something better close at hand. He could see the glint of the metal work on bridles, the vague outlines of saddles, and one glistening spot of moonlight on the rump of a horse. Half a dozen of them were tethered in one group among the trees just before him.

"Dave! Dave!" yelled the searchers.

"Here," groaned the feeble voice of the deputy.

MacTee stepped to the tethered mustangs, chose the biggest for himself, mounted it, untied the others of the group, and led them off at a quiet walk that turned into a jangling trot, and thence into a flying gallop that swept him straight toward the Dormer Pass.

XI

The horses of Harrigan and Katie Malone were already entering the thick mist. At once they were lost as though in smoke. Above them the strength of the moon pierced here and there through the gathering storm clouds. It peered as though through a window, and sent down a broad shaft of milky white enabling the two riders to see one another, vaguely.

The way had grown extremely steep. The horses began to slip and slide. Even mountain horses, which are nearly sure-footed as goats, could hardly negotiate those smooth rocks after the wet of the clouds had greased them.

They rode very close together, for a time. Then Harrigan dismounted. His great bulk made it difficult for his horse to climb. The girl, however, could still make better progress by remaining in the saddle.

It began to be difficult work. In half a dozen places, the horses could barely climb the sharp grades. They grunted. Their striking, sliding hoofs knocked long sparks out of the stones. And yet through this difficult time, they did not speak to one another. Not until Kate said, as they paused a moment, panting: "Do you think that we were right to take this pass?"

"Molly seems to be right about everything. She told us to take this one," answered Harrigan.

"Aye, but suppose that MacTee is able to make her talk to him, and gets the name of the pass out of her, and the fact that we've gone through this way?"

"You don't know MacTee," said Harrigan. "He's man enough to smash a regiment, but he couldn't even whisper against a woman." He added, out of the largeness of his heart: "There's only one thing I regret, and that is that I didn't go find him myself before I left Yellow Gulch."

As he spoke, looking toward the girl, a radiance of moonlight flowed over her through the mist and made her like a form of glowing marble.

She said: "All right, Danny. We don't care, so long as we're here together, and safe for the minute. Only . . . ."

"Only what?" urged Harrigan.

"It's too happy," she answered. "It can't last. There's a pricking in my blood that tells me. There's something that follows me like a ghost."

They had come to a narrow point of the ravine, as she spoke, and here the wind gathered as into a funnel, blew the mist rushing against their faces, then dispersed it as the wind gathers the dust of the desert and sweeps it off against the horizon.

They looked back to find that the pass was clear of mist, for the moment, behind them. And that was how they happened to see, far away, laboring up the slope of a very distant incline, the form of a horseman who looked larger than human, the horse driven frantic by constant spurring.

"MacTee," said Harrigan.

He felt, in an instant, as though he were a small child followed by a demoniacal power. The very thought of MacTee became overpowering.

"Angus MacTee!" cried the girl. For even at that distance she, also, could recognize the bearing and size of the Black MacTee.

They looked at one another, silently. There was no longer a mist between them. They could see each other's face clearly, and as plainly as he could see the fear in the face of the girl, so she could see the fear in the face of Harrigan.

They fled up the pass, the hoofs of the horses striking out an iron clangoring.

Then the wind ceased. The clouds closed over them more darkly than ever. The moonlight ceased. They began to fumble forward through a wet, cold darkness.

Wind came again, but it did not clear away the clouds. It merely heaped on more and more mountainous vapors. Gusts of rain struck them wetly in the darkness. The hail came in great, pelting volleys of stones that dazed and hurt the horses. They whacked on the broad shoulders, they stung and cut the face of Harrigan, until he almost wondered that the girl could keep in her saddle.

But she made no complaint.

He dismounted again, went to her during a brief halt, and took her hands. They were as ice. He made her bend down from the saddle, and he kissed her face. It was icy, also. All her body was quivering. He knew that it was not the storm but the fear that was killing her, and he wanted to say words that would start the currents of her blood again. But he was not able to speak.

He went on, leading the two horses, with an ache of emptiness in his heart. He knew that he was afraid, and he feared lest she might despise him for the terror that he felt.

The storm increased. The wind came charging. Under the weight of it and the sting of the hail and rain that charged it, the horses frequently halted and balked.

The moon shone through again briefly. Harrigan saw the mouth of a ravine that opened to the right, and into this he suddenly turned.

Now the high walls shut off the main torrent of the storm. The clouds flowed higher over them, and only occasional rattlings of hail beat against them. Then the hail ceased, and it rained in torrents. The lightning sprang with it, making the mountain faces above them fluctuate wildly.

It was by the lightning that he saw how the girl had bowed herself, clinging to the saddle pommel with both hands, her head down, as one who submissively endures, without hope.

He felt as though he had beaten her. He felt as though she were a child.

The next moment, they turned a narrow bend in the ravine, and the valley widened before them. The heavier roaring that he had thought to be the mere thundering of the wind, he knew, now, to be the dashing of water. And on the edge of the cañon wall, he saw a small shack and shed, built together, of logs.

He made for that. It was a steep and treacherous slope that they had to cover to get to the cabin. It was so steep and covered with loose, rolling stones, that it seemed incredible that anyone should have built in such a spot. Something must have altered the place in the meantime. The slope must have increased with weathering, and the treacherous coating of loose stones, like so many ball bearings, must have rolled down from the upper part of the mountain.

They came to the cabin doorway, in which there was no door. A blare of lightning showed them that there was nothing but a bleak emptiness within the place.

They entered, and the regular pulsing of the lightning showed them the vacant hearth, three broken chairs, and a loft of small poles overhead, with a ladder leading up to the attic trap door.

Harrigan climbed the ladder, tore down some of the poles, and came to the floor again. He broke up the poles and one of the chairs. Of the smallest fragments of the woods, he made a heap of tinder that had splintered off from the larger pieces. This he was able to light with his fourth match.

The yellow finger of flame took hold, mastered bit after bit of the refuse, burned up strong and clear. He built up the fire, cording the larger pieces around the flame.

Now the pale flare of the lightning was not the only illumination. There was, besides, the steadier, smokier light from the fire.

This showed to Harrigan the drooping figure of the girl. She stood close to the wall, one hand resting against it. He went to her and touched her shoulder.

She looked up to him. Her head fell back. She looked like one about to die.

"He could see the firelight," said Kate.

Harrigan studied her a moment. She was dripping wet, so that her clothes clung to her, and she looked amazingly helpless. It was not that he loved her less, but for the moment it seemed an amazing thing that two forces as great as Harrigan and MacTee should be engaged in mortal combat because of such a negligible thing.

Yet there was no question that she was worth more than the rest of the universe to both of them. They knew her of old.

But she was crushed and weak, now. She was not the independent, strong, and almost imperious creature she had been. Strength had gone from her with hope, and Harrigan knew why. It was because she felt that terrible events lay just around the corner from them.

Harrigan felt the same thing. It was a sense of inevitable and inescapable disaster.

"He would see the house, if he happens to turn down this ravine after us," said Harrigan. "But there's no reason why he should come this way. He'll go on through the pass, against the storm. That's the way of MacTee. He faces things. He fights them straight through. That's the greatness of him. Nothing turns him back. But if he happens to come through the ravine toward us, the lightning would show the cabin to him. The firelight won't matter."

"We'd better go on, then," said the girl in a rapid, broken voice. "I don't want to stay here. It's like a cavern. I'd rather die in the open, than in a house . . . ."

He put his hand against her face. It was burning hot. Despair ran through him in a sickening current.

Yet he made his voice calm to answer: "We'll have to stay here. As a matter of fact, there's no way of getting through without the danger of your catching pneumonia. I don't dare take you through this sort of weather."

"I won't melt," she said. She laughed a little, and repeated: "I won't melt."

It was like the voice of a child, trying to be brave. It was like the piping voice of a child. The heart of Harrigan was wrung by the sound of it.

"I'm taking the horses into the shed, the poor devils," he said to her. "You stay in here and take your clothes off. Take them off and wring them dry. Look at you. You're soggy. You're wet to the skin. Wring your clothes as dry as you can and drag them on again. I'll stay with the horses in the shed till I've fixed myself the same way."

She looked at him vaguely, as though she had not understood.

"Do you have to go away, Danny?" she said. "I don't want you to go away. Stay here with me."

He was incredulous. He never had seen her so childish. Had the fever affected her mind? No, the dilation of her eyes gave the answer. It was not the heat fever, but the intense cold of fear that had numbed her brain. Her lips were pale. Her eyes were as great as the eyes of an owl. He would hardly have recognized her face.

"Do what I tell you, Kate," he said sternly. He talked like a father to a child. "Do what I tell you. Take off your clothes and wring them out. I'll be in the shed. Look. You tap on this partition, and I'll be back in here before even a lightning flash would be able to jump in and steal you away from me."

"All right," said the girl. "It's all right."

She was actually smiling, a crooked, wistful smile.

Harrigan mastered his heart and went outside. The rain blasted against his face. The roar of it was less than the sound inside the cabin, but every water drop cut at his skin.

The two horses were huddled against the wall of the house, shrinking from the sweep of the storm, and wincing from the strong glare of the lightning. Overhead, the thunder broke in an endless booming, like the water of a great cataract falling on a world of tin.

Harrigan pulled at the reins. The horses closed their eyes and stretched out their necks, without stirring, for a moment. Then they followed him to the shed.

No water entered it, and no wind. A musty smell of emptiness was there, and some of the warmth of the day that had not yet ebbed away.

Harrigan stripped off his clothes. He was glad to give his strength to something. He almost tore the tough fabrics to pieces by the power with which he twisted them. Then he dragged them on again.

He took a bandanna, rolled it, and used that to rub down the horses until they were fairly dry. Their body heat set them steaming. By the lightning flashes he could see the steam rising. The rank smell of their damp pelts filled the little shed.

Suddenly the rain stopped beating. He looked out and discovered that the southern half of the sky was thronged with the great black forms of the storm, with lightning leaping beneath it. But in the northern portion of the sky there were enormous white waves of clouds, with the moon riding through them. It struck a solid bank, was lost in it, then burst through, flinging a luminous spray before it. Harrigan drew in his breath. The weight of the thunder, also, was withdrawn from his brain, as it were.

He hurried around to the front of the cabin. As he strode, the stones rolled suddenly under his weight. He was thrown flat, and skidded down the sharp incline until, at the very verge of the cañon, he found a fingerhold, and stayed his fall.

From where he lay, he could look down a hundred yards of cliff that was almost sheer to where a river worked and whirled and leaped white in the bottom of the gorge.

He remained prone for an instant, waiting for his heart to stop racing. Then he got up, cautiously, and crawled to the cabin before he ventured to rise and go weak-kneed to the doorway.

Beside it, he called: "Kate!"

"Yes!" she answered.

"Are you through? May I come in?"

"Come in," she replied.

He paused to look down the ravine. A wisp of mist was standing in it like a monstrous ghost. Otherwise, it was empty, the moonlight glistening over the wet rocks.

Then he stepped inside and found the girl seated in a broken chair beside the fire. Her clothes were fitted to her skin as sleekly as the pelt of a wet animal. She had not followed his instructions. And she looked up at him with the same dumb, suffering eyes of fear.

XII

He crouched beside her. Bent in that fashion, he felt far more keenly the hugeness of his bulk compared with her.

"What is it, Kate?" he asked.

She shook her head.

"It's MacTee," he insisted. "You're afraid of MacTee. You think that he's sure to come."

She closed her eyes.

"Well," said Harrigan, "you can't sit here in wet clothes. You'll have to do something about it. You'll have to wring them out, Kate. I told you that. Listen to me . . . if you won't do anything . . . if you just give up like a child . . . I'll have to undress you and wring out the clothes myself."

She opened her eyes and stared at him, as one who cannot understand.

He thought he would startle her into alertness. So he put out his hand and unfastened the top button of her khaki shirt. No change came in her uncomprehending eyes.

"Kate!" he exclaimed. "For God's sake, what's the matter?"

She closed her eyes again. The firelight touched her face, gently. The smoke, hardly drawn up the chimney at all from the hearth, curled behind her, and she was as the stuff of which dreams are made.

"It's MacTee," she answered. "Ever since the old days, I've been afraid, Danny. I've always known that a time would come when he and you would meet for the final time. I've always known, and now . . . ."

"Now what?" asked Harrigan, staring in his turn, for the whole affair had grown ghostly.

She was silent. He touched her face. It was flushed and still burning hot. Her hands were hot, too, and dry. When she looked at him, there was a film over her eyes. A terrible feeling grew up in him that her brain was giving way under the strain.

"It's going to be all right," said Harrigan. "There's been enough to keep us apart. This is the last bad time . . . this night, the storm, and all of that. Afterwards, we're going to have plane sailing."

"Not on this earth," whispered her lips.

A ghostly coldness stole through his blood. He wanted to ask her if she had the power of second sight.

She said more loudly: "I know it's the end, Danny. I want to make the most of it. I want to be gay. I want to make you happy for the last time. But I can't. There's a shroud over me. I'm afraid. I'm buried alive in fear."

"It's because you've been thinking of MacTee too long," said Harrigan. "You've made a ghost out of him. That's all. Besides, you're too excited. And it's night. The minute the sun comes up you'll forget all of this. Everything will be all right."

She lifted her head to answer, but, instead of speaking, she stared with terrible eyes of fear past him, toward the door.

Then the heavy, booming voice of MacTee said: "Everything will be all right for her, Harrigan. But you or I will be dead!"

Harrigan rose to his feet slowly, like an old man whose joints are frozen by age.

He turned. And there in the doorway, filling it from top to bottom, stood MacTee. His clothes were glued to his body by the wet. The brim of his sombrero sagged heavily around his face. And the face itself was as Harrigan had seen it before, in times of settled passion, like gray iron. The storm had not affected him, any more than it could affect a steel beam.

"Come out," said MacTee.

A revolver was held in his right hand, waist high. Harrigan studied it. He was far faster with a gun, far straighter in the shooting of it. Perhaps there was a ghost of a chance that he would be able to get out a weapon and end the thing with a bullet.

MacTee said: "Don't try it, Harrigan. Don't try it."

And Harrigan knew that it would be folly to try.

He looked back at the frozen face of the girl.

"Maybe this is the end, Kate," he said. "Maybe you've been seeing the future a lot more clearly than I can make it out."

He leaned and kissed her good bye. Her face had been burning before. Now it was cold. She made no response. Harrigan was not in her eyes at all, but only the great body and the terrible face of MacTee.

Harrigan turned to the door and strode toward it. MacTee backed away from the entrance. Harrigan had stepped outside when the girl screamed suddenly, a frightful sound, as though a bullet had torn through her flesh.

Harrigan glanced back. He saw that she had not risen from the chair. She simply sat as before, but with her head thrown back like a dying thing.

He stepped on into the night. The storm had retreated farther away. It was so far away, now, that the voices in it could hardly be heard, and over the rest of the sky fled the shining white waves of clouds with the moon sweeping grandly through them.

MacTee still backed up, step by step. Harrigan followed him to a little distance from the hut. Then MacTee stopped and glanced around him, swiftly—very swiftly, for fear lest the least absence of care might enable the magic of Harrigan to produce a gun.

Then he said: "Hoist your hands, Harrigan."

His voice had the clang of iron in it.

Harrigan threw his hands well above his head. He knew that he was in touching distance, in breathing distance, of death.

"Turn your back to me!" commanded MacTee.

Harrigan turned his back. That was the hardest thing to do, to turn one's back on a nightmare terror. But he turned his back, little by little.

MacTee stepped up to him and laid the weighty muzzle of the revolver in the small of Harrigan's back.

"If you make a move . . . if you even breathe," said MacTee, "I'll blow your spine in two."

"I won't move," said Harrigan.

The hand of MacTee searched him. It found two revolvers and threw them away. It found a knife, and threw it away.

The pressure of the gun was removed. MacTee drew back. "Turn around again," he said.

Harrigan turned.

MacTee weighted the Colt in his hand.

"I ought to kill you like a dog," he said. "You went into Yellow Gulch to search for both of us. You found Kate. You told her enough lies to get her for yourself. Then you got hold of the deputy sheriff and told him where to find me. You're a traitor. You're a treacherous dog, and I ought to shoot you like a dog. But killing with a bullet wouldn't do me much good. I'm going to use my hands on you, Harrigan. I'm going to kill you with my hands."

He tossed the revolver away and spread out his great hands.

"It's been coming to you for a long time," said MacTee. "And now you're going to get it."

"I didn't send the deputy sheriff," said Harrigan honestly. "I'm not such a sneak. I sent a girl to let you know . . . ."

"My God," shouted MacTee, "are you going to try to lie out of it like a dirty dog? Are you going to turn yellow when the pinch comes?"

And as he spoke, he rushed in at Harrigan.

Harrigan struck with all his might. His fist glanced as on rock, but he was able to side-step the rush. He turned and met it again. After the first blow, his heart was working again.

"I'm going to tear you to bits," said MacTee, wiping the blood from his face.

"MacTee," said Harrigan, "there never was a time when a Scotchman could beat an Irishman. It's the end of you, damn you. Come in and take it."

MacTee laughed. It was a terrible thing to watch, and a terrible thing to hear, that laughter of MacTee. And he came in again, with a leap.

There was no stopping him. Harrigan knew it. He hammered in a long, over-arm punch that landed solidly in the face. Then he doubled over quickly and got a low hold, straightened, and heaved the weight of MacTee over his shoulder.

The hand of MacTee gripped at him. With one gesture it tore coat and shirt from his back. Harrigan saw the white flash of the moon on his body. He looked down, and glimpsed the corrugated strength of his muscles, and laughed in turn. The battle madness had entered him.

He ran in as MacTee arose, and shouted: "Now, MacTee! Now, Angus! We'll see who's the better man!"

So he plunged straight into the embrace of MacTee.

He had reason to regret it, the instant later. For the arms of MacTee were iron, hot iron, that shrank into place around Harrigan and crushed him. The power of a machine squeezed the breath from Harrigan.

In a sudden panic, he beat at the head and at the body of MacTee. He saw that it was as idle as splashing drops of water off a rock. His wind was almost gone. He tried for another grip by shooting his right arm under the armpit of MacTee and bending his forearm over the shoulder. By chance he fixed his grasp on the point of MacTee's jaw. The flesh was no more than a thin masking for the bone. It was against the bone that the grip of Harrigan was biting.

In the meantime, his own breath was gone. He jerked with all his might. The face of MacTee was convulsed to the mask of a beast, a dead beast, glaring with eyes of glass from the wall of a hunting lodge. The great neck muscles of MacTee bulged out to meet the strain. His whole body shook as Harrigan jerked with all his might, again and again, striving to bend back the erect head.

There was a sudden giving. The head of MacTee had gone back an inch, another inch. He groaned in an agony. They turned slowly. Bit by bit the head of MacTee was going back. His body began to bend at the waist. His knees sagged. He became smaller than Harrigan. He tottered. He was about to fall, but that was not enough for Harrigan, who suddenly shifted his clutch lower. The great spread of his fingers, like talons, fastened across the throat of MacTee.

That was the end. He held the life of the man. A bubbling, gasping sound came from MacTee's lips. He staggered this way and that. It was a miracle that his stalwart legs still could hold him up, when he was dying on his feet.

Dying—all that was MacTee now pinching out in darkness, all the lion of courage and savage cruelty and great hearted friendship, also diminishing like a light that will fail and can never be kindled again.

"Angus!" groaned Harrigan. "I can't be murdering you, man." He added: "Say that you've had enough . . . I can't be murdering you."

But he knew, as he said this, that it was a vain appeal, for Black MacTee had never surrendered before, and he would never surrender now. How could that nature admit defeat?

Suddenly Harrigan loosened his grasp. "I can't do it, MacTee!" he groaned, drawing back.

He had been in so close that there was no chance for those hammering bludgeons, the fists of MacTee, to strike a vital spot.

But drawing away, he came into perfect range. At the last instant, he saw the danger coming like a shadow, from the corner of his eye. He tried to raise his left arm to block the punch. But his hasty guard was beaten down. A ponderous mass struck full and fair on the side of his chin, near the point. The shock was telegraphed into his brain like a thunderclap, while the darkness of thunderclouds spread over his eyes.

The moonlight seemed to disappear. Before him all was the thick of night.

In that murk of darkness, he saw a vague silhouette drifting. He put up his hands and stretched them out. But terrible blows struck him and knocked across his brain showers of fiery sparks. They gave him only light by which to see his own coming destruction. He was beaten, and he knew that he was beaten.

A wave of sick weakness came over him. He fell on hands and knees. The darkness, at the same time, cleared instantly from his mind, letting in the fullness of the moonlight, so that he could see the valley, the pale boat of the moon, the clouds that fled down the wind.

He saw MacTee, in the act of catching up a great, jagged stone, and heaving it into the air.

A sudden lightness of body and a strength of limb enabled Harrigan to rise. Once upon his feet, he could only stand there, tottering, his helpless arms hanging at his sides.

He saw the stone heaved back, until the strain of the effort was shown in the whole body of MacTee, prepared to deal the final stroke.

But MacTee did not strike. The stone dropped out of his hand and thumped its weight heavily against the ground.

"Damn you, Harrigan," said MacTee, "I can't do it. You're a traitor, Harrigan. But I can't finish you off the way you deserve to be finished."

Harrigan pointed toward the cabin.

"It's the girl that counts, MacTee. She's half out of her mind with fear of you. We've got to show ourselves to her . . . alive."

He stumbled forward. His knees were so uncertain that he was in danger of falling. MacTee gripped him by the arm and sustained him. They moved forward crookedly toward the cabin.

"Why did you do it, Harrigan?" asked MacTee. "Why did you knife me in the back? Why did you tell 'em where to hunt me down?"

"I didn't," said Harrigan. "I'll swear on the Book, MacTee, that I left a girl behind to take the news to you that I was gone, and Kate with me. Maybe she was afraid to go and thought she'd do better by sending men and guns. I don't know. But I wouldn't stab you in the back, MacTee . . . as you've tried to stab *me*, many a time."

"You lie," said MacTee.

He released the arm of Harrigan. And Red Harrigan, giving his head a shake, turned like a bull on MacTee.

"All down the railroad line, you left the railroad dicks ready to put lead in me. Answer me that, MacTee."

"Are you going to bring up the past?" asked MacTee gloomily. "Are you going to . . . ?"

A faintly murmuring voice broke in upon them from the cabin.

"Hush," said MacTee. "Do you hear?"

They hurried into the cabin, and there they found that the girl was slumped against the wall of the shack, her head fallen on one shoulder, her eyes closed, her face crimsoned with more than the heat of the firelight.

MacTee put his hand on her forehead.

"She's burning with the fever, Danny!" gasped MacTee. "Ah, Harrigan, what have I done?"

Harrigan brushed him aside. It was not hard to do. There seemed to be no strength remaining in MacTee, for the moment.

Harrigan pressed his face against her breast and heard the rapid hammering of her heart.

"It's the shock that's made her sick, Angus," he said. "And happiness will make her well, again. I'm sure of that. Make her know that we're friends."

"Friends?" said MacTee. "I'd rather be friends to a snake than to a Harrigan."

"You fool," said Harrigan. "Do you think that *I* want your friendship? I wouldn't have the whole man of you, not a dozen a nickel. But it's the girl that I'm thinking of. Make her know that you're not hounding the trail of her and me, now."

MacTee stared sourly at the red-headed man. Then he leaned and called: "Kate! Kate Malone! Oh, Kate, do you hear me?"

She opened her eyes and looked uneasily toward him. Fear began to gather in her face.

"Hush, Kate," said MacTee. "Here's Dan Harrigan beside me. Do you see that? And we're friends, Kate. We'll be friends all the days of our life. There's nothing to be afraid of."

She looked blankly at him.

"Is it true, Danny?" she said.

"It's true," said Harrigan.

"Then let me sleep again," said the girl. "I haven't slept . . . I haven't dared to rest . . . for years and years . . . ."

"Oh, God," said MacTee. "What have I done, if she dies, Harrigan?"

"I'll tell you, MacTee," said Harrigan.

"Tell me, then," said Angus MacTee, "and curse me, Dan. Damn my heart black, because black it is."

"You're talking like a fool, MacTee," said Harrigan. "What's in a man has to come out of him. You loved her too much to want to see her turned over to a man like me, that's all. I'm not worthy of her. Neither are you. God pity her for coming into the hands of either of us, Angus. But God knows you're a better man than I am. If there's a black devil in you, there's a red devil in me."

"You're raving, Danny," said MacTee. "It hurts me to see you make such a fool of yourself. Stay here with her. Hold her life in your hands like a young bird, and I'll be back with a doctor to take care of her for you."

Instantly he was gone through the door of the cabin. The galloping hoofs of his horse went ringing up the valley and faded away into nothingness.

XIII

It was a long, long night for Dan Harrigan. He climbed the rock to the wooded mountainside above and broke off evergreen branches until he had enough arm loads of them to make a bed. He beat them dry, built them soft and thick in the cabin, near the fire, and spread a saddle blanket over them. There he put the girl.

She merely groaned in her sleep as he lifted her. Another saddle blanket covered her. Harrigan sat beside her and watched through the hours.

Her breathing grew easier and more regular, and deeper. Another light than the red of the fire began to enter the cabin, and, turning his head, Harrigan saw the doorway brightened by the coming of the day.

A greater hope came up in Harrigan at the same time. He went to the door and stared out at the dawn, which was brightening the mountains above them.

"Dan!" called a voice behind him.

He whirled about and found her sitting up, braced on both arms.

"I've been dreaming," said the girl. "I thought that MacTee came."

"Hush," said Harrigan. "He came, and he's gone again. He'll never trouble us again."

He heard the clattering hoofs of horses coming down the valley, over the rocks. So he went to the doorway, and, looking out, he saw three riders, of whom the first was MacTee.

As they came up, Harrigan saw that the other two were elderly men, frowning with grave thoughts and with the labor of their ride into the mountains. They dismounted.

"Two would be better than one, for what's wrong with Kate," said MacTee. "Here's Doctor Harden."

"She's better," said Harrigan to the doctor. "She's a lot better. I think the fever's dead in her."

The doctor gave him a rather biting glance, then entered the cabin.

Harrigan remained outside with the other two.

"It's a strange business," said the other visitor, shaking his head. "What the law will say to this kidnapping in the middle of the night . . . what the law will say to that, you know as well as I do, Mister MacTee."

"Let the law be damned," said MacTee. "There are things above the law, I can tell you. And one of them is Harrigan and MacTee, just now."

The voice of the doctor spoke from within.

"She wants to see both of you . . . Harrigan and MacTee."

They entered.

Her face was half white and half flushed. Eagerly she fixed her glance upon MacTee.

"Is it true, Angus?" she asked. "Are you the friend of Dan Harrigan now, and always?"

MacTee scowled at Harrigan, but he nodded.

"Was there ever a man made for a better friend than Harrigan?" he said. "I'll tell you this, Kate. I came up last night to find him and murder him. We fought it out. He could have choked the life out of me, Kate. He had my life in the tips of his fingers, but he wouldn't take it. And then the chance came to me. I had him helpless, and I couldn't finish him. There's a charm on us,

Kate. We can't harm one another. And if you want him, you want the better man of us."

"Take his hand, then, Angus," said the girl.

"Here, Danny," said MacTee.

He turned and gripped the ready hand of Harrigan.

"I wish to God that I'd never laid eyes on you, Dan," said MacTee. "But now that it's too late for such wishing, I hope to the same God that nothing will ever come between us again."

"Why," said Harrigan, "Angus, if we put our hands together, not even the devil could tear 'em apart. And there's my hand for life."

"Kiss me, Danny," said the girl. "God bless the two of you. This is the happiest day the world ever saw. Kiss me, Angus, too."

MacTee leaned over her.

"It's a way of kissing good bye to what I've wanted the most in my life," he said. "But there you are, Kate." He touched his lips to her forehead. "I've kissed one part of you good bye, but not the friend in you, Kate."

"No," she said, with sudden tears running down her face. "Never that."

"Come in here, now!" exclaimed MacTee, rising. "I brought two doctors . . . to make all well. I'm going to see an end of this damned business and get it off my mind for good. Come in here, Johnson."

The solemn face of the other stranger appeared in the doorway.

"Here's a sky pilot," said MacTee. "He'll tie your hand into the hand of Harrigan. I'm going outside till the trick's turned. Afterwards, I'm coming back inside to see what Missus Danny Harrigan looks like, and how she wears her new name!"

He strode out through the doorway.

"You must make him happier, Danny," said the girl. "Make him come back and be our witness. Can you lead him back in here?"

"Can I?" said Harrigan joyously. "Why, I could lead him now with a silk thread. I could lift the whole weight of the soul of him on the tip of my little finger. For didn't you see, Kate? The blackness has gone out of MacTee forever!"

THE END

About the Author

Max Brand is the best-known pen name of Frederick Faust, creator of Dr. Kildare, Destry, and many other fictional characters popular with readers and viewers worldwide. Faust wrote for a variety of audiences in many genres. His enormous output, totaling approximately 30,000,000 words or the equivalent of 530 ordinary books, covered nearly every field: crime, fantasy, historical romance, espionage, Westerns, science fiction, adventure, animal stories, love, war, and fashionable society, big business and big medicine. Eighty motion pictures have been based on his work along with many radio and television programs. For good measure he also published four volumes of poetry. Perhaps no other author has reached more people in more different ways. Born in Seattle in 1892, orphaned early, Faust grew up in the rural San Joaquin Valley of California. At Berkeley he became a student rebel and one-man literary movement, contributing prodigiously to all campus publications. Denied a degree because of unconventional conduct, he embarked on a series of adventures culminating in New York City where, after a period of near starvation, he received simultaneous recognition as a serious poet and successful author of fiction. Later, he traveled widely, making his home in New York, then in Florence, and finally in Los Angeles. Once the United States entered the Second World War, Faust abandoned his lucrative writing career and his work as a screenwriter to serve as a war correspondent with the infantry in Italy, despite his fifty-one years and a bad heart. He was killed during a night attack on a hilltop village held by the German army. New books based on magazine serials or unpublished manuscripts or restored versions continue to appear so that, alive or dead, he has averaged a new book every four months for seventy-five years. Beyond this, some work by him is newly reprinted every week of every year in one or another format somewhere in the world.